中西節慶文化英語

Eastern & Western Festivals

Pei-Chin Hsieh / Owain Mckimm

Eastern & Western Festivals

CONTENTS MAP

	UNIT	READING 閱讀

New Year's Day
新年

I Reading   🎧 01

    "Happy New Year!" is an **expression**[1] you'll hear a lot on January 1, the day when most people in the West celebrate **the beginning of** a brand-new year. The celebration of New Year is one of the oldest traditions in the world. It was first **observed**[2] by the **ancient**[3] **Babylonians** about 4,000 years ago. However, unlike the modern-day New Year, the Babylonian New Year began in the spring. This may seem strange to many Westerners, but when you consider that spring is the season of **rebirth**,[4] it is in fact quite **logical**.[5]

In 153 BC, the **Romans** were the first in Europe to select January 1 as New Year's Day because that was the day when newly elected[6] officials[7] **took office**. The rest of Europe continued to celebrate New Year in spring until 1582, when Pope Gregory XIII made some changes to the old calendar. The celebration of New Year was officially moved to January 1 because the **Pope** named the first day of this new calendar New Year's Day.

1. **expression** [ɪkˋsprɛʃən] (n.) 表達；措辭
2. **observe** [əbˋzɝv] (v.) 慶祝（節日）
3. **ancient** [ˋenʃənt] (a.) 古老的
4. **rebirth** [riˋbɝθ] (n.) 再生；復活
5. **logical** [ˋlɑdʒɪkl] (a.) 合邏輯的；合理的
6. **elected** [ɪˋlɛktɪd] (a.) 當選的；選上的
7. **official** [əˋfɪʃəl] (n.) 官員

★ **Babylonian** [ˌbæbɪˋlonjən] (n.) 巴比倫人
★ **Roman** [ˋromən] (n.) 羅馬人
★ **Pope** [pop] (n.) 教宗

phr. **the beginning of** ……的開始
phr. **take office** 官員就職

▼ancient Babylonians

▲Pope Gregory XIII

「新年快樂！」是國曆一月一日時常聽見的一句話。這一天中，大多數西方人都會慶祝嶄新一年的開始。慶祝新年是世界上最古老的節慶活動之一，約四千年前，巴比倫人率先慶祝新年。然而，不像現代的新年，巴比倫人的新年始於春季，許多西方人可能會對此感到奇怪，但只要想到春季是重生的季節，其實還頗有邏輯的。

西元前 153 年時，羅馬人是歐洲最早選擇一月一日成為元旦的民族，因為那天是新科官員的就職日。其餘的歐洲國家都於春季慶祝新年，直到 1582 年教宗額我略十三世更改了舊制曆法後才有所改變。在教宗將新曆第一天立為元旦後，人們正式將新年的慶祝活動移到一月一日。

Nowadays, people all around the world throw parties to see in the New Year. In the United States, more than a million people visit Times Square in New York City to see the famous "Times Square Ball Drop," and those who can't be **present**[8] often watch the event on TV.

At 10 seconds before midnight, the countdown begins: Ten, nine, eight, seven, six . . . And as the clock strikes 12, whistles are blown, people honk car horns, fireworks are set off, and everyone cheers and kisses his or her loved ones (or sometimes even a stranger).

In addition, it is traditional at this time for people to make New Year's **resolutions**.[9] These are often personal **objectives**,[10] such as planning to lose weight or quit smoking. Now, you may wonder when making New Year's resolutions became a **tradition**.[11] You guessed it! It was 4,000 years ago with the ancient Babylonians!

▼New Year's Eve countdown at Times Square

8. **present** [`prɛznt] (a.) 出席的
9. **resolution** [ˌrɛzəˈluʃən] (n.) 決心；決定
10. **objective** [əbˈdʒɛktɪv] (n.) 目標
11. **tradition** [trəˈdɪʃən] (n.) 傳統；慣例

phr. **in addition** 除此之外

現在世界各地的人們會舉辦派對以迎接新年。在美國，超過一百萬人會前往紐約市的時代廣場去看知名的「時代廣場降球儀式」，而無法親自到場的人們則通常會透過電視觀賞該活動。

在午夜前十秒鐘時，人們會開始倒數：十、九、八、七、六……。當午夜鐘聲響起，人們會吹起哨子、鳴響汽車喇叭並放起煙火，大家都高聲歡呼並親吻親朋好友（有時候甚至會親吻陌生人）。

除此之外，在這個時刻立下新年新希望是項傳統。這些新希望通常是個人目標，像是計劃減肥或戒菸。你現在可能想知道立下新年新希望是在何時成為傳統的，你猜的沒錯，這跟 4,000 年前的古巴比倫人有關！

II Reading Comprehension Questions

( ) **1.** When was the earliest celebration of New Year?
    a Four hundred years ago.
    b In 153 BC.
    c Four thousand years ago.
    d In 1582.

( ) **2.** Why did the Romans choose January 1 as New Year's Day?
    a It began a season of rebirth.
    b It was more logical.
    c It was the day that new officials took office.
    d It was what the Pope ordered.

( ) **3.** Whom began the tradition of making New Year's resolutions?
    a Pope Gregory XIII.
    b The Romans.
    c The Americans.
    d The Babylonians.

( ) **4.** Who or what do people in America kiss at the stroke of midnight on New Year's Eve?
    a A ball.
    b Their loved ones.
    c The ground.
    d Their cars.

( ) **5.** Which of the following is likely to be a New Year's resolution?
    a I will save more money.
    b I love New Year.
    c I shouldn't have cheated on the exam.
    d Happy New Year!

New Year, **NEW YOU**

Conversation

NEW YEAR'S RESOLUTIONS

Danny So, Joan. What are your New Year's resolutions this year?

Joan I've just made one this year. It's to watch less TV and read more books.

Danny Oh, that's a good one. My friend made a **similar**[1] resolution last year. He decided to read a book a week for the **whole**[2] year.

Joan Did he **manage**[3] it?

Danny No, I think he **kept** it **up** for about six months and then got too busy.

Joan Well, six months isn't bad. That's longer than most people manage to keep their resolutions! So, what are yours?

Danny I just made one as well. My resolution is to exercise more. I got a new bike for Christmas, so I'm going to try cycling every day.

Joan Well, good luck with it!

1. **similar** [ˋsɪmələ] (a.) 相似的
2. **whole** [hol] (a.) 全部的；整個的
3. **manage** [ˋmænɪdʒ] (v.) 設法做到；勉力完成

phr. **keep up** 保持

10

新年新希望

丹尼：所以瓊恩，妳今年的新年新希望是什麼？

瓊恩：我今年只有一個新希望，我希望能少看點電視多讀點書。

丹尼：喔，還不錯啊，我朋友去年也有類似的新希望，他希望一整年能每週讀一本書。

瓊恩：那他成功了嗎？

丹尼：沒有，他持續了大約六個月，接著就太忙了。

瓊恩：六個月也頗厲害的，比大多數人守住新希望的時間還長，那麼你的新希望是什麼呢？

丹尼：我也只有一個，我的新希望是多運動。我聖誕節時得到一台新腳踏車，我會試著每天都去騎車。

瓊恩：那麼，祝你好運囉！

IV Listening Practice

 03

( ) **1.** Which of the following does David NOT ask Jenny?

　　[a] Whom she's going to kiss at midnight.

　　[b] If she's enjoying the party.

　　[c] What time it is.

　　[d] What her New Year's resolutions are.

( ) **2.** According to the dialogue, how much time is left until midnight?

　　[a] Five minutes.

　　[b] Thirty minutes.

　　[c] One hour.

　　[d] Five hours.

( ) **3.** Where will the speakers go next?

　　[a] To the TV room.

　　[b] To the roof.

　　[c] To a window.

　　[d] To the kitchen.

Chinese New Year
中國新年

I Reading

04

Chinese New Year (also known as Lunar New Year or Spring Festival) is the most important of all the traditional Chinese holidays. Unlike Western New Year, which always takes place on January 1, Chinese New Year follows the **lunar**[1] calendar and thus falls somewhere between late January and mid-February.

The **origins**[2] of Chinese New Year are lost in time, but an interesting **myth**[3] describes how the festivities supposedly began. **According to** the story, there was once a **village**[4] in China that was being **terrorized**[5] by a lion-like **beast**[6] called the *Nian*. **In an attempt to** save their village, the villagers **set off firecrackers**, hoping that the loud noise would scare the monster away. They also **hung up** red **lanterns** and stuck red

▲ lion dance

strips of paper with lucky sayings written on them around their doors. After that, the Nian never **bothered**[7] the villagers again. People still perform these actions today **in remembrance of** the event.

1. **lunar** [ˈlunɚ] (a.) 陰曆的;農曆的
2. **origin** [ˈɔrədʒɪn] (n.) 起源
3. **myth** [mɪθ] (n.) 神話
4. **village** [ˈvɪlɪdʒ] (n.) 村莊
5. **terrorize** [ˈtɛrə͵raɪz] (v.) 使懼怕
6. **beast** [bist] (n.) 野獸
7. **bother** [ˈbɑðɚ] (v.) 打擾

★ **firecracker** [ˈfaɪr͵krækɚ] (n.) 鞭炮
★ **lantern** [ˈlæntɚn] (n.) 燈籠
★ **strip** [strɪp] (n.) 狹長的一條或一片

▼ firecrackers

phr. **according to** 根據
phr. **in an attempt to** 企圖
phr. **set off** 施放
phr. **hang up** 掛
phr. **in remembrance of** 紀念

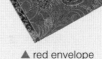

▲ red envelope

　　中國新年(也稱作農曆新年或春節)是所有傳統中國節日中最重要的節日。不像西洋新年總在一月一日慶祝,中國新年隨著農曆變動,落於一月底到二月中之間。

　　中國新年的源由隨著悠久歷史而難以考證,但有個有趣的神話解釋了此節慶可能的起源。根據傳說,以前中國曾有某個村落被長得像獅子的年獸所迫害,為了拯救村莊,村民們施放鞭炮,希望巨大聲響會把年獸嚇跑,他們也掛上紅色燈籠並在大門邊貼上寫了吉祥話的紅紙。從此之後,年獸不再擾民,而人們直至今日仍進行這些活動以紀念這個事件。

◀ writing lucky sayings on red strips of paper

In all, the New Year celebrations **last**[8] for more than two weeks, and each day has a special activity **associated**[9] with it. On the first day of New Year, for example, younger family members go and visit older **relatives**[10]; on the second day, married women return to their pre-marital home, and so on. The biggest day of celebrations, however, is New Year's Eve. On this day, families come together for a big **reunion**[11] dinner. Special foods that **symbolize**[12] wealth and **prosperity**,[13] such as **dumplings**, chicken, and **clams**, are always eaten, along with *chang nian cai*, or long-year vegetables, which symbolize long life and good health. After dinner, young children are given red envelopes filled with money from their parents, while older parents receive similar red envelopes from their grown-up children. But the party doesn't stop there. On New Year's Eve, everyone stays up late playing mahjongg, eating snacks, and **launching**[14] fireworks well into the early hours of the morning.

8. **last** [læst] (v.) 持續

9. **associate** [əˈsoʃɪ‚et] (v.) 與……有關

10. **relative** [ˈrɛlətɪv] (n.) 親戚；親屬

11. **reunion** [riˈjunjən] (n.) 團聚

12. **symbolize** [ˈsɪmbḷ‚aɪz] (v.) 象徵

13. **prosperity** [prɑsˈpɛrətɪ] (n.) 興旺；昌盛；成功

14. **launch** [lɔntʃ] (v.) 發射

★ **dumpling** [ˈdʌmplɪŋ] (n.) 水餃

★ **clam** [klæm] (n.) 蛤蜊

　　總而言之，新年的慶祝活動總共持續超過兩個禮拜，而且每天皆有與之相關的特別活動。舉例來說：第一天是新年，年輕的家庭成員會去造訪長輩，而第二天已婚的女性會回娘家，其他日子也類似如此。不過，最盛大的慶祝日是除夕，在這天，家人會聚在一起吃頓豐盛的團圓晚飯。晚飯中有些特別的食物象徵財富和興隆，像是水餃、雞肉和蛤蠣都是常見的菜餚，而長年菜則代表長壽和健康。晚餐後，父母會給年幼的孩童裝著錢的紅包，而較年長的父母則會從成年子女那裡收到紅包。但慶祝不會就此結束，大家在除夕時都會晚睡、打麻將、吃零食或放煙火，這會一直持續到凌晨。

▲ dumplings

II Reading Comprehension Questions

(   ) **1.** On which of the following dates could Chinese New Year fall?

     [a] January 1.

     [b] January 27.

     [c] March 11.

     [d] June 5.

(   ) **2.** What is the Nian?

     [a] A lion-like monster.

     [b] A lucky vegetable.

     [c] A village in China.

     [d] A wise old man.

(   ) **3.** Who gets red envelopes on New Year's Eve?

     [a] Teachers, doctors, and policemen.

     [b] People who work in the service industry.

     [c] Young children and parents with grown-up children.

     [d] Newly married couples.

(   ) **4.** What do dumplings represent when eaten during Chinese New Year?

     [a] Long life.

     [b] Good health.

     [c] Wealth.

     [d] Intelligence.

(   ) **5.** Which of the following does NOT happen on New Year's Eve?

     [a] The whole family eats a big dinner.

     [b] Everyone stays up late.

     [c] People set off fireworks.

     [d] Married women visit their parents.

(III) Conversation

05

CHINESE NEW YEAR TABOOS

Xiao Ming Sarah, breakfast is ready.

Sarah OK. I'll just take a quick shower, and I'll be right down.

Xiao Ming All right, but don't wash your hair, OK?

Sarah What? Why not?

Xiao Ming Today is New Year's Day. If you wash your hair today, you'll wash away all your luck for the coming year.

Sarah Oh, right. Is there anything else I should **avoid**[1] doing today?

Xiao Ming Well, you mustn't use any scissors or knives; if you do, you'll cut off all your good luck. You mustn't **sweep**[2] the floor either; if you do, all your good luck will be swept away.

Sarah I see. Anything else?

Xiao Ming Yes, don't **lend**[3] anyone any money. If you do, you'll be lending people money all year.

1. **avoid** [əˈvɔɪd] (v.) 避開；避免
2. **sweep** [swip] (v.) 打掃；掃除
3. **lend** [lɛnd] (v.) 借出

▲ reunion

16

農曆新年禁忌

小明：莎拉，早餐準備好了。

莎拉：好的，等我迅速洗個澡就下去了。

小明：好的，但不要洗頭髮喔。

莎拉：什麼？為什麼不行？

小明：今天是新年，若妳今天洗頭髮，會把來年的好運都洗掉。

莎拉：喔是喔，那有其他我今天要避免做的事嗎？

小明：嗯，妳不能使用剪刀或刀子，如果妳使用了，會切斷所有的好運。妳也不能掃地，因為這麼做會把好運掃出門。

莎拉：了解，還有其他的嗎？

小明：還有，不要把錢借給別人，若妳這樣的話，整年都只有把錢借給別人的運。

 **Listening Practice** 06

(　) **1.** Why is the couple going to the temple?

    ⓐ To receive a blessing.

    ⓑ To ask a god's advice.

    ⓒ To borrow money.

    ⓓ To get their fortunes told.

(　) **2.** With whom do they need to make peace?

    ⓐ The temple's owner.

    ⓑ The Year God.

    ⓒ Their ancestors.

    ⓓ Their friends.

(　) **3.** In which year were the two born?

    ⓐ The Year of the Rat.

    ⓑ The Year of the Dog.

    ⓒ The Year of the Horse.

    ⓓ The Year of the Dragon.

Lantern Festival
元宵節

I Reading

07

The 15th and final day of the Chinese New Year holidays is **marked**[1] by the Lantern Festival. This is the time of year when colorful lanterns light up the night sky and everyone eats bowls upon bowls of *tangyuan*—chewy balls made of rice flour that symbolize togetherness and family unity. The lanterns seen at the Lantern Festival come in all shapes and sizes. Some are small, round, and red; others are **gigantic**,[2] multicolored, and shaped like the animals of the Chinese **zodiac**. In addition to these **decorative**[3] lanterns, people also **send off** sky lanterns, which are made of thin paper and have an **opening**[4] at the base where a small fire is **suspended**.[5] People write their wishes for the future on these lanterns and then send them flying high into the sky like mini **hot air balloons**.

There are many **legends**[6] about the origins of Lantern Festival. One of these is that the festival originated with Qin Shi Huang, the **emperor**[7] who first united China. It is said that the emperor held the first Lantern Festival **in order to** honor[8] the ancient god of heaven, Taiyi, hoping that the happiness and joy created by the Lantern Festival would make the god listen to his **prayers**.[9]

▼ Chinese Zodiac

rat
ox
tiger
rabbit
dragon
snake
horse
goat
monkey
dog
rooster
pig

▶ tangyuan

1. **mark** [mɑrk] (v.) 標記；表明
2. **gigantic** [dʒaɪˈgæntɪk] (a.) 巨大的；龐大的
3. **decorative** [ˈdɛkərətɪv] (a.) 裝飾性的
4. **opening** [ˈopənɪŋ] (n.) 開口
5. **suspend** [səˈspɛnd] (v.) 懸掛
6. **legend** [ˈlɛdʒənd] (n.) 傳說；傳奇故事
7. **emperor** [ˈɛmpərə] (n.) 皇帝

8. **honor** [ˈɑnə] (v.) 使榮耀
9. **prayer** [prɛr] (n.) 禱告；祈願

★ **zodiac** [ˈzodɪˌæk] (n.) 黃道帶
★ **hot air balloon** [hɑt ɛr bəˈlun] (n.) 熱氣球

phr. **send off** 施放
phr. **in order to** 為了……

　　元宵節在大年初十五，也就是農曆新年假期的最後一日。在這時節，色彩繽紛的燈籠將點亮夜空，人們也會吃一碗接著一碗的「湯圓」——由糯米粉製成且有嚼勁的球狀食物，象徵家人團圓。元宵節的燈籠有五花八門的形狀與尺寸，有些是較小的圓形紅燈籠，有些則是以十二生肖動物為造型的巨大彩色燈籠。除了這些裝飾性的燈籠之外，人們也會施放天燈。天燈由薄紙製成，底部有開口以懸掛火苗。人們會將對未來的願望寫在天燈上，並讓它們像小型熱氣球一樣飛向高空。

　　與元宵節起源相關的故事有很多，其中一說和秦始皇有關，他是第一位統一中國的皇帝。根據傳說，這位皇帝舉行第一次的元宵節為了要祭祀天帝太乙，希望元宵節歡欣喜樂的氣氛能讓太乙神聆聽他的祈求。

◀ send off a sky lantern

Another story tells of a beautiful bird that flew down to Earth from heaven and was killed by some villagers. It just so happened that this bird was the favorite of the Jade Emperor, who ruled heaven. In his anger, the Jade Emperor **ordered**[10] that the village be **destroyed**.[11] Hearing of the god's plan, the villagers went into a **panic**[12]; luckily for them, a wise man came up with a **cunning**[13] plan to save the village. He advised the villagers to **explode**[14] firecrackers and light lanterns so that, from heaven, it would look like the village was already burning. Amazingly, the plan worked, and the Jade Emperor ordered his **troops**[15] to **stand down**. From then on, the villagers lit lanterns every year on the same day to remember their lucky escape.

10. **order** [`ɔrdɚ] (v.) 命令
11. **destroy** [dɪ`strɔɪ] (v.) 毀壞；殺死
12. **panic** [`pænɪk] (n.) 恐慌
13. **cunning** [`kʌnɪŋ] (a.) 狡猾的；奸詐的
14. **explode** [ɪk`splod] (v.) 使爆炸；使爆破
15. **troop** [trup] (n.) 部隊

phr. **stand down**（軍隊）撤退

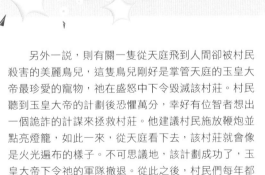

◀ explode firecrackers

　　另外一說，則有關一隻從天庭飛到人間卻被村民殺害的美麗鳥兒，這隻鳥兒剛好是掌管天庭的玉皇大帝最珍愛的寵物，祂在盛怒中下令毀滅該村莊。村民聽到玉皇大帝的計劃後恐懼萬分，幸好有位智者想出一個詭詐的計謀來拯救村莊。他建議村民施放鞭炮並點亮燈籠，如此一來，從天庭看下去，該村莊就會像是火光遍布的樣子。不可思議地，該計劃成功了，玉皇大帝下令祂的軍隊撤退。從此之後，村民們每年在這天點亮燈籠以紀念這幸運逃過一劫的日子。

II Reading Comprehension Questions

( ) **1.** When is Lantern Festival celebrated?
- a The first day of the Chinese New Year holidays.
- b In the middle of the Chinese New Year holidays.
- c At the end of the Chinese New Year holidays.
- d After the Chinese New Year holidays have ended.

( ) **2.** Why do people release sky lanterns?
- a To apologize to the Jade Emperor.
- b To wish for a good future.
- c To complain about their families.
- d To give thanks for the good things in their lives.

( ) **3.** According to one legend, why did Qin Shu Huang hold the first Lantern Festival?
- a He wanted to please the god of heaven.
- b He wanted to honor his ancestors.
- c He wanted to impress his people.
- d He wanted to scare away evil spirits.

( ) **4.** According to the final paragraph, how did the wise man save the villagers from Jade Emperor's anger?
- a He gave them weapons to defend themselves.
- b He told them how to trick the Jade Emperor.
- c He showed them a safe place to hide.
- d He convinced the Jade Emperor to be merciful.

( ) **5.** When someone "goes into a panic," what are they NOT?
- a Nervous.
- b Afraid.
- c Calm.
- d Bothered.

(((▶ Conversation

08

GUESSING LANTERN RIDDLES

Jane   Why is everyone gathered outside that temple, Xiao Wang?

Xiao Wang   They're guessing lantern **riddles**.[1] You see that guy on the stage? He reads out riddles, and people have to try and guess the answer.

Jane   Do you get something if you guess the correct answer?

Xiao Wang   Yeah, you get a red envelope or a small gift.

Jane   I want to try and guess one.

Xiao Wang   OK, the clue is "A big king with two **horns**.[2]"

Jane   Um . . . That's **tricky**.[3] I have no idea. Do you know the answer?

Xiao Wang   Someone just shouted it out. The answer is "Beautiful."

Jane   I don't get it.

Xiao Wang   It's because the Chinese **character**[4] for "beautiful" looks like the characters for "big" and "king," with two little horns on top.

Jane   Oh, right. I think these riddles are going to be too **tough**[5] for me!

1. **riddle** [ˈrɪdl] (n.) 謎語
2. **horn** [hɔrn] (n.) 角
3. **tricky** [ˈtrɪkɪ] (a.) 有考驗性的
4. **character** [ˈkærɪktɚ] (n.) 中文字
5. **tough** [tʌf] (a.) 困難的

猜燈謎

珍妮：小王，為什麼大家都聚集在那個寺廟外呢？
小王：他們在猜燈謎。看到那個站在台上的人嗎？
　　　他會說出謎題，而人們則會試著猜出答案。
珍妮：如果答對的話有獎品嗎？
小王：有啊，妳會得到紅包或是小禮物。
珍妮：我想試著猜一題看看。
小王：好啊，謎題是「大王頭上長兩角」。
珍妮：嗯……有點難，我不知道耶，你知道答案嗎？
小王：有人剛喊出答案了，答案是「美」。
珍妮：我不懂。
小王：因為「美」這個中文字看起來很像是「大」
　　　和「王」的結合，上面再加上像角的兩小撇。
珍妮：喔，也對，我覺得這些謎題對我而言太難了！

IV Listening Practice 🎧 09

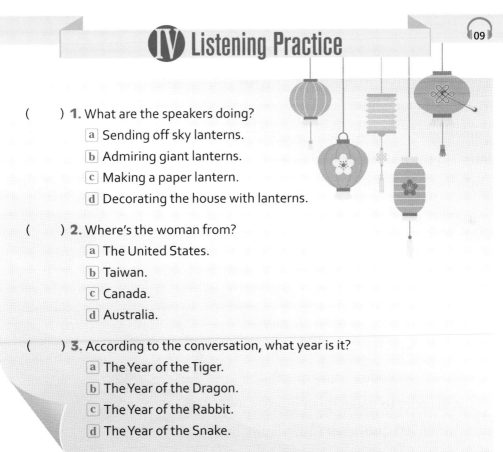

( ) **1.** What are the speakers doing?
　　a Sending off sky lanterns.
　　b Admiring giant lanterns.
　　c Making a paper lantern.
　　d Decorating the house with lanterns.

( ) **2.** Where's the woman from?
　　a The United States.
　　b Taiwan.
　　c Canada.
　　d Australia.

( ) **3.** According to the conversation, what year is it?
　　a The Year of the Tiger.
　　b The Year of the Dragon.
　　c The Year of the Rabbit.
　　d The Year of the Snake.

Valentine's Day
西洋情人節

I Reading

🎧 10

Have you ever wondered why the holiday for lovers in the West is called Valentine's Day? Or why most Valentine's cards are signed[1] with the phrase "From your Valentine"? Or why Cupid is a popular symbol[2] used on Valentine's Day? The answers to all these questions can be found in the customs[3] and beliefs[4] of ancient Rome and in the legend of a third-century saint.

Long before Valentine's Day was observed, the Romans used to worship[5] a pagan god called *Lupercus*. A three-day festival was held to honor the god on the 13th, 14th, and 15th of February. During this festival, young men would strip naked[6] and smack[7] the bottoms of young women with whips in order to make them more fertile.[8] In AD 496, after Christianity had become dominant,[9] the Church decided to

Cupid ▶

make February 14 a saint's day in order to **replace**[10] the still-popular yet **uncivilized**[11] festival of Lupercus. They decided to **dedicate**[12] the day to St. Valentine, who was **beheaded**[13] in AD 269 for secretly marrying young men and women when marriage was **banned**[14] by the Roman Emperor Claudius.

1. **sign** [saɪn] (v.) 簽名
2. **symbol** [ˋsɪmb!] (n.) 符號；象徵
3. **custom** [ˋkʌstəm] (n.) 社會習俗
4. **belief** [bɪˋlif] (n.) 信仰；信念
5. **worship** [ˋwɝʃɪp] (v.) 崇拜；祭祀
6. **naked** [ˋnekɪd] (a.) 赤裸的
7. **smack** [smæk] (v.) 打
8. **fertile** [ˋfɝt!] (a.) 有生育力的
9. **dominant** [ˋdɑmənənt] (a.) 佔優勢的

10. **replace** [rɪˋples] (v.) 取代
11. **uncivilized** [ʌnˋsɪvl͵aɪzd] (a.) 不文明的
12. **dedicate** [ˋdɛdə͵ket] (v.) 奉獻；獻給
13. **behead** [bɪˋhɛd] (v.) 砍頭
14. **ban** [bæn] (v.) 禁止

Roman Emperor Claudius ▶

你曾經想過為什麼西方的情人節被稱為「Valentine's Day（華倫泰日）」嗎？或是為什麼大多數情人節卡片署名時都有這個詞彙「From your Valentine（妳的華倫泰之筆）」？或為什麼邱比特是情人節受歡迎的象徵圖像？這些答案都源自古羅馬的習俗和信仰，還有西元第三世紀的聖人傳奇。

早在人們還沒開始慶祝情人節之前，羅馬人祀奉一位異教神祇盧波庫斯，並在二月 13 日、14 日和 15 日時舉辦為期三天的慶典以敬拜這位異教神。在這場慶典中，年輕男子會赤身裸體並用鞭子鞭打年輕女子的臀部，使其增進生育能力。在西元 496 年時，基督教已成為主要宗教，而教會決定將二月 14 日訂為聖人之日，取代仍然盛行但卻不文明的盧波庫斯慶典。他們決定將此日用來紀念華倫泰聖人，他在西元 269 年被砍頭，因為他在羅馬克勞狄烏斯皇帝禁止婚姻時，秘密為一對年輕男女證婚。

The story also goes that while in prison **awaiting**[15] death, St. Valentine fell in love with his jailer's blind daughter and **cured**[16] her blindness. On the eve of his beheading, he wrote the woman a note and signed it "From your Valentine," which later became a popular phrase for Valentine's cards.

Nowadays, Valentine's Day is a chance for couples to express their love and for people to seek the **affection**[17] of those they **admire**.[18] Lovers **exchange**[19] chocolates, flowers, gifts, and Valentine's cards, which are often decorated with a drawing of Cupid, the Roman god of **desire**.[20] It was said that whoever got hit by one of Cupid's arrows would **be filled with** an uncontrollable love for the first person he or she **laid eyes on**.

15. **await** [əˋwet] (v.) 等待
16. **cure** [kjur] (v.) 治療
17. **affection** [əˋfɛkʃən] (n.) 情誼；鍾愛
18. **admire** [ədˋmaɪr] (v.) 欽佩；欣賞
19. **exchange** [ɪksˋtʃendʒ] (v.) 交換
20. **desire** [dɪˋzaɪr] (n.) 渴望

phr. **be filled with** 充滿……
phr. **lay eyes on** 注意；心儀

▲ exchange

這個故事也相傳在華倫泰聖人坐牢等待死刑之際，他與典獄長的失明之女相戀並治好她的眼疾，在行刑前一晚，他寫信給該名女子並署名「妳的華倫泰之筆」，從此之後這成為情人節卡片常用的署名方式。

現在的情人節是情人們互表愛意或對欽佩之人表達好感的機會，情人們會互贈巧克力、花朵、禮物和情人節卡片。情人節卡片上通常有邱比特的裝飾圖案，邱比特是羅馬愛神。相傳被邱比特弓箭射到的人，將對第一眼見到的人充滿無法自拔的傾慕之意。

II Reading Comprehension Questions

( ) **1.** Nowadays, for whom is Valentine's Day a holiday?

    a Couples in love.

    b Parents and their children.

    c Teachers.

    d Worshipers of Lupercus.

( ) **2.** How did St. Valentine die?

    a He committed suicide for love.

    b He was beheaded for committing a crime.

    c He died of an illness.

    d He was murdered by his wife.

( ) **3.** In prison, St. Valentine fell in love with a girl. What couldn't she do?

    a Speak.

    b See.

    c Hear.

    d Love.

( ) **4.** According to the passage, which of these is sometimes exchanged between lovers on Valentine's Day?

    a Money.

    b Chocolates.

    c Figures of St. Valentine.

    d Arrows.

( ) **5.** Who is Cupid?

    a The brother of St. Valentine.

    b An Olympic archer.

    c The emperor who ordered St. Valentine's death.

    d The Roman god of desire.

🎧 Conversation

MAKING A VALENTINE'S DAY RESERVATION

Hostess Hello. This is Ratatouille. How may I help you?

Leo I'd like to make a **reservation**[1] for Valentine's Day. Are there still tables **available**[2]?

Hostess Yes, we still have some tables available. Would you like to book a table for two?

Leo Yes, please. That would be great. Is 7:30 OK?

Hostess That's no problem, sir. We actually have a special Valentine's set menu that includes an **appetizer**, an **entrée**, a **dessert**,[3] and a glass of wine for $20 per person. Would you like me to put you down for that? Or would you like to eat from the **regular**[4] menu?

Leo The set menu sounds great. Put us down for that.

Hostess All right, sir. Now if I can just have your name and phone number . . .

1. **reservation** [ˌrɛzəˈveʃən] (n.) 預訂
2. **available** [əˈveləbl̩] (a.) 可得到的；有空的
3. **dessert** [dɪˈzɜt] (n.) 甜點
4. **regular** [ˈrɛgjələ] (a.) 一般的

★ **appetizer** [ˈæpəˌtaɪzə] (n.) 開胃菜
★ **entrée** [ˈɑntre] (n.) 主餐

RESERVED

reservation ▶

appetizer ▶

entrée ▶

◀ dessert

預約情人節大餐

女侍：哈囉，法式燉菜小館，請問您需要什麼服務？

李奧：我想要預訂情人節大餐，請問還有位子嗎？

女侍：有的，我們還有一些位子，請問您要訂一張兩
　　　人桌嗎？

李奧：好的，謝謝，太好了，請問七點半可以嗎？

女侍：先生，沒問題，我們其實有提供特別的情人套
　　　餐，包括一份開胃菜、一份主餐、一份甜點
　　　和一杯酒，一個人是 20 元。您要我幫您預約
　　　這份套餐嗎？或是您想直接點一般的餐點？

李奧：套餐聽起來很棒，幫我們預訂吧。

女侍：好的先生，現在請您給我您的大名和電話號
　　　碼……

Ⅳ Listening Practice 🎧 12

(　　) **1.** What does the man ask the woman for?

    a A Valentine's Day card.

    b Some ideas for Valentine's Day.

    c A restaurant recommendation.

    d A date on Valentine's Day.

(　　) **2.** What did the man do for Valentine's Day last year?

    a He took his girlfriend away for the weekend.

    b He gave his girlfriend a box of chocolates.

    c He made a CD of romantic songs for his girlfriend.

    d He proposed to his girlfriend.

(　　) **3.** What is the man going to do for Valentine's Day this year?

    a Write a romantic song.

    b Write a love poem.

    c Cook a romantic meal.

    d Buy a piece of expensive jewelry.

St. Patrick's Day
聖派屈克節

I Reading

If you live in Asia, the **shamrock**—a common low-growing plant with three heart-shaped leaves on each **stem**[1]—probably doesn't mean much to you. But show a shamrock to a Westerner, and the first thing that will **pop into** his or her **mind** is "St. Patrick's Day!"

Celebrated on March 17 each year, St. Patrick's Day is the day when the people of Ireland **commemorate**[2] their **patron** saint. And in other parts of the world, St. Patrick's Day has **evolved**[3] into an **ethnic**[4] holiday celebrating Irish **heritage**,[5] especially in places with a significant Irish **immigrant**[6] **population**,[7] such as the United States.

But nowhere in the world does the holiday **bustle**[8] with more noise and excitement than Dublin, the Irish **capital**.[9] Dublin's St. Patrick's Festival, the largest St. Patrick's Day celebration in the world,

Guinness® ▶

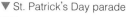
▼ St. Patrick's Day parade

abounds with **carnival**-style **parades**,[10] spectacular fireworks, and outdoor dance events. People dress in green (the color of Ireland) from top to toe, drink Guinness® (Ireland's signature dark beer), and dance and sing from morning to night. But who was St. Patrick, and why is he so important to the Irish?

1. **stem** [stɛm] (n.) 莖
2. **commemorate** [kəˋmɛməˌret] (v.) 慶祝；紀念
3. **evolve** [ɪˋvɑlv] (v.) 演變
4. **ethnic** [ˋɛθnɪk] (a.) 種族上的
5. **heritage** [ˋhɛrətɪdʒ] (n.) 遺產；傳統
6. **immigrant** [ˋɪməgrənt] (a.) 移民的

7. **population** [ˌpɑpjəˋleʃən] (n.) 人口
8. **bustle** [ˋbʌsl̩] (v.) 充滿
9. **capital** [ˋkæpət!] (n.) 首都
10. **parade** [pəˋred] (n.) 遊行

★ **shamrock** [ˋʃæmrɑk] (n.) 三葉草
★ **patron** [ˋpetrən] (n.) 庇護者
★ **carnival** [ˋkɑrnəv!] (n.) 嘉年華會

phr. **pop into mind** 映入腦海

◀ St. Patrick

▲ shamrock

若你住在亞洲，三葉草可能對你而言沒有什麼意義。三葉草是一種矮小的植物，每根莖上都長著三片心形的小葉子。倘若你給西方人看三葉草，第一個湧上他／她念頭的是「聖派屈克節」。

聖派屈克節於每年三月 17 日舉行，是愛爾蘭人紀念主保聖人的日子。在世界其他地方，聖派屈克節已演變成為慶祝愛爾蘭傳統的民族節慶，在愛爾蘭移民人口眾多的地方尤甚，例如美國。

但世上再也沒有其他地方，比愛爾蘭首都都柏林用更震耳欲聾的聲響和熱情迎接這個節慶。全世界最盛大的聖派屈克節慶祝活動是都柏林的聖派屈克慶典，充滿嘉年華式的遊行、壯觀的煙火和戶外舞蹈活動。人們從頭到腳會身著綠色服裝（愛爾蘭的代表色），飲用健力士啤酒（愛爾蘭的著名黑啤酒），並從早到晚歌舞不歇。但是，聖派屈克到底是誰？他又為何對愛爾蘭人如此重要？

St. Patrick was the man who, in the 5th century, introduced Ireland to Christianity and successfully **transformed**[11] the country into a Catholic nation. St. Patrick's gift was that he could explain **complicated**[12] things to people in ways that were easy for them to understand. <u>**For example**</u>, he used the common shamrock in his **sermons** to explain to people the **concept**[13] of the Christian **Trinity**—that God is three separate persons but is still only one God. He said the shamrock's three leaves **represented**[14] God the Father, God the Son, and God the Holy Spirit—all separate but joined to form a whole. The shamrock became the saint's symbol, and its green color became representative of the saint, the holiday, and then Ireland itself.

11. **transform** [træns`fɔrm] (v.) 改變
12. **complicated** [`kɑmplə͵ketɪd] (a.) 複雜的；難懂的
13. **concept** [`kɑnsɛpt] (n.) 概念
14. **represent** [͵rɛprɪ`zɛnt] (v.) 代表；呈現

★ **sermon** [`sɝmən] (n.) 講道
★ **Trinity** [`trɪnətɪ] (n.) 三位一體

phr. **for example** 舉例來說

Trinity ▶

在西元五世紀時，聖派屈克將基督教引進愛爾蘭，並成功地將其轉化為天主教國家。聖派屈克的天賦是他能用簡明易懂的方式解釋複雜的事物以讓人們了解。舉例來說，他在講道中用常見的三葉草向會眾解釋基督教三位一體的概念──神是一位有三種位格的唯一真神。三葉草的三片葉子代表神的三種位格，聖父、聖子和聖靈，他們有不同的形象，卻又能合而為一成為一體。三葉草成為這位聖人的代表符號，而綠色則先成為此聖人的象徵色，接著代表節慶，最後成為愛爾蘭的代表色。

II Reading Comprehension Questions

( ) **1.** Which of these colors is most likely to be seen on St. Patrick's Day?

    a Gray.

    b Green.

    c Blue.

    d Red.

( ) **2.** Which of these activities does NOT happen as part of St. Patrick's Day celebrations in Dublin?

    a Parades.

    b Fireworks.

    c Gift giving.

    d Dancing.

( ) **3.** According to the passage, what did St. Patrick do all across Ireland?

    a Preach Christianity.

    b Set up businesses.

    c Organize festivals.

    d Heal the sick.

( ) **4.** Why is the shamrock associated with St. Patrick's Day?

    a Because it was St. Patrick's favorite food.

    b Because in Irish, "shamrock" sounds similar to "Patrick."

    c Because St. Patrick used it in his teachings.

    d Because St. Patrick wore one in his hat.

( ) **5.** In which of these cities would you most likely see a St. Patrick's Day parade?

    a New York city.

    b Bangkok.

    c Macau.

    d Mexico City.

Conversation

ST. PATRICK'S DAY CELEBRATIONS

Billy   Are you going to the St. Patrick's Day Festival in town tomorrow, Maggie?

Maggie   Yes, definitely! I can't wait.

Billy   Me either. I've never been to a St. Patrick's Day Festival before.

Maggie   Oh, you'll love it! First, there's the parade, which is so much fun. They have marching bands, dancers, street performers—and they're all dressed in traditional Irish costumes.

Billy   Sounds amazing. What **route**[1] does it take?

Maggie   It goes from the end of Main Street all the way to the town square.

Billy   And then after the parade has finished?

Maggie   When the parade has finished, they have an all-day festival in the **square**.[2] There are **food stalls**[3] and a big stage for performances. I think they've even invited a famous Irish **comedian**[4] to do a show this year.

1. **route** [rut] (n.) 路線
2. **square** [skwɛr] (n.) 廣場
3. **food stall** [fud stɔl] (n.) 小吃攤販
4. **comedian** [kə'midɪən] (n.) 喜劇演員

34

聖派屈克節慶祝活動

比利：瑪姬，妳明天會去市區的聖派屈克節嗎？

瑪姬：會啊，當然囉，我等不及了。

比利：我也是，我以前從沒參加過聖派屈克節的慶典。

瑪姬：喔，你一定會很喜歡的，會先有遊行，超好玩的。遊行會有遊行樂隊、舞者和街頭藝人，他們都會穿著傳統愛爾蘭服飾。

比利：聽起來真是太讚了，他們的遊行路徑是什麼？

瑪姬：會先從主要大街尾端一直走到市區廣場。

比利：那麼遊行結束後呢？

瑪姬：遊行結束之後，在廣場有整天的慶祝活動，會有小吃攤和表演大舞台，我想他們今年好像還邀請了一位知名的愛爾蘭喜劇演員來表演。

 **IV Listening Practice** 15

( )**1.** Why is the man concerned?

    a He can't find his green wig.

    b The woman won't go with him to the parade.

    c The woman isn't wearing the right clothes.

    d He doesn't know what time the parade starts.

( )**2.** What is the man wearing around his shoulders?

    a A towel.

    b A tablecloth.

    c A scarf.

    d A flag.

( )**3.** Which of these opinions is expressed by the woman?

    a Wearing wigs is cool.

    b Green doesn't suit her.

    c The man is dressed smartly.

    d Standing out from the crowd is important.

Easter Day
復活節

 **I Reading**

16

Easter is a Christian holiday celebrated by believers throughout the Western world. According to the Bible, Jesus Christ was **crucified** on Good Friday. He then **rose**[1] from the dead two days later on Easter Sunday, also called Easter Day. In fact, Easter has become so **rooted**[2] in Western culture that many people **participate**[3] in Easter activities **regardless of** whether they're Christian or not.

Parents often give their children delicious chocolate eggs or **arrange**[4] Easter egg **hunts**[5] in the garden. (These eggs, the children are told, were hidden there by a magical rabbit called the *Easter Bunny*.) Sometimes villages will even hold egg-rolling competitions, with eggs being **rolled**[6] downhill in a race. In Greece, eggs are **dyed**[7] red to symbolize the blood of Christ, while in some Eastern European countries, they are painted with **intricate**[8] and beautiful designs.

Many of these Easter traditions, however, predate Christianity. There is some **evidence**[9] to suggest that the ancient **tribes**[10] of Northern Europe celebrated the coming of spring by worshiping their fertility goddess, Eostre. The rabbit, or **hare**, was her symbol because these creatures were known to be particularly fertile. Eggs were also once a common symbol of spring because they symbolized new life. Now, though, they symbolize the empty **tomb**[11] of Christ.

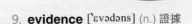
▲ Easter egg hunt

1. **rise** [raɪz] (v.) 上升
2. **rooted** [ˈrutɪd] (a.) 根深蒂固的
3. **participate** [pɑrˈtɪsəˌpet] (v.) 參加
4. **arrange** [əˈrendʒ] (v.) 安排
5. **hunt** [hʌnt] (n.) 尋找
6. **roll** [rol] (v.) 滾動
7. **dye** [daɪ] (v.) 染色
8. **intricate** [ˈɪntrəkɪt] (a.) 錯綜複雜的

9. **evidence** [ˈɛvədəns] (n.) 證據
10. **tribe** [traɪb] (n.) 部落；種族
11. **tomb** [tum] (n.) 墳墓

★ **crucify** [ˈkrusəˌfaɪ] (v.) 釘十字架
★ **hare** [hɛr] (n.) 野兔

phr. **regardless of** 不管；不顧

　　復活節是基督教的節日，西方世界的信徒都會歡慶這個日子。根據《聖經》，耶穌基督在週五受難日被釘上十字架而死，但兩天後他於週日復活節由死裡復活。事實上，由於復活節已在西方文化中根深蒂固，不管是否為基督徒，許多人都會參與復活節活動。

　　父母通常會給孩童可口美味的巧克力蛋，或在院子安排尋找復活節蛋的遊戲，家長會告訴孩子們，這些蛋是被稱為復活節兔的神奇兔子所藏匿。有時候村莊甚至會舉辦滾蛋大賽，比賽誰能將蛋最迅速地滾下山坡。在希臘，蛋會被染成紅色以代表基督的聖血，而其他東歐國家則將蛋塗上精美的圖案。

　　有許多復活節的傳統甚至可追溯至基督信仰之前，有些證據顯示北歐的古老部落會膜拜生育女神厄俄斯，以慶祝春天的到來，而兔子或野兔則是她的象徵符號，因為這些動物以繁殖力強而知名。蛋以前常也曾是春天的代表，因為它象徵新生命，不過在現今，蛋象徵了耶穌基督的空墳墓。

◀ being crucified

The forty-day period that leads up to Easter is called *Lent*, a period of self-discipline, prayer, and **contemplation**.[12] During this time, some strict Christian groups <u>**swear off**</u> any kind of animal products. More relaxed believers, on the other hand, simply <u>**give up**</u> one or two **beloved**[13] items of food, such as cakes or candy. Either way, because it marks the end of this period of **disciplined**[14] eating, Easter is a time of feasting and celebration. It's no surprise, then, that in the United Sates, Easter is **arguably**[15] the most candy-crazed holiday of the year. More than $2 billion is spent annually on **goods**[16] such as chocolate bunnies, **marshmallow** chicks, and jelly beans!

▼ Easter eggs

12. **contemplation** [ˌkɑntɛmˈpleʃən] (n.) 沈思；冥想
13. **beloved** [bɪˈlʌvɪd] (a.) 心愛的
14. **disciplined** [ˈdɪsəplɪnd] (a.) 遵守紀律的
15. **arguably** [ˈɑrgjʊəblɪ] (adv.) 可以認為
16. **goods** [gʊdz] (n.) 商品

★ **marshmallow** [ˈmɑrʃˌmælo] (n.) 棉花糖

phr. **swear off** 發誓戒除
phr. **give up** 放棄

marshmallows ▶

▲ chocolate bunny

　　復活節前 40 天被稱為大齋期，人們會自我約束、禱告並冥想。在這期間，一些恪守戒律的基督教團體會完全禁食肉類；另一方面，較不嚴謹的教徒只會戒掉一或兩樣喜歡吃的食物，像是蛋糕或糖果。不管如何，由於復活節代表這段禁食時間的結束，因此是饗宴與狂歡的時刻。這也難怪在美國，復活節可被稱為一年當中人們對糖果最感到瘋狂的節日，每年都有超過 20 億美元被花在購買巧克力兔、棉花糖小雞和雷根糖。

◀ Lent

II Reading Comprehension Questions

(　) **1.** Who participates in Easter activities?
- a Only Christians.
- b Only non-Christians.
- c Both Christians and non-Christians.
- d Only Eastern Europeans.

(　) **2.** Which of the following is another name for Easter Day?
- a Good Friday.
- b Easter Sunday.
- c Eostre Day.
- d Candy Sunday.

(　) **3.** In Greece, what does the red dye used to color Easter eggs symbolize?
- a Blood.
- b Happiness.
- c Wealth.
- d Good fortune.

(　) **4.** From which event do many Easter traditions originate?
- a An American festival of chocolate.
- b A Greek saint's day celebration.
- c A pre-Christian spring festival.
- d An Eastern European festival of art.

(　) **5.** Which of these traditions is associated with Lent?
- a Painting eggs with interesting designs.
- b Giving up certain types of food.
- c Having egg-rolling races.
- d Spending lots of money on candy.

III Conversation

17

HIDING EASTER EGGS

Paul OK, we need to find a good place to hide these Easter eggs.

Ruth How about we hide a few in this rosebush?

Paul Good idea. Actually, why don't we hide some in all of the flower **bushes**[1]?

Ruth Yeah, OK. Put red eggs **among**[2] the red flowers, blue eggs among the blue flowers, and so on.

Paul **Scatter**[3] some of the green eggs on the lawn, too.

Ruth What if the kids **stamp**[4] on them by accident?

Paul Hmm . . . OK, hide the green eggs in the branches of that tree, among the leaves.

Ruth Done. Now, where should we put the giant egg?

Paul Oh! I Know! Hide it under that **empty**[5] flowerpot.

Ruth OK, all set. Let's go and call the kids.

bush ▶

1. **bush** [buʃ] (n.) 灌木叢
2. **among** [əˋmʌŋ] (prep.) 在……之中
3. **scatter** [ˋskætɚ] (n.) 分散；散布
4. **stamp** [stæmp] (v.) 踩；踏
5. **empty** [ˋɛmptɪ] (a.) 空的

藏復活節蛋

保羅：好，我們得找個地方把這些復活節蛋都藏起來。

茹絲：我們藏一些在這玫瑰叢裡如何？

保羅：好主意，其實我們何不把所有蛋都藏在花叢裡呢？

茹絲：好啊沒問題，把紅色的蛋藏在紅花叢裡，藍色的蛋藏在藍花叢裡，其他也類似這樣。

保羅：也把一些綠色的蛋分散藏在草坪中。

茹絲：如果小朋友不小心踩到怎麼辦？

保羅：嗯……好吧，把綠色的蛋藏在那棵樹的樹枝，藏在葉子裡面。

茹絲：藏好了，那大顆的蛋要放哪？

保羅：喔！我知道！把它藏在那個空的花盆裡。

茹絲：好，一切就緒，我們去叫小朋友來吧！

 **Listening Practice** 18

( ) **1.** What does the woman suggest they do for Easter?

    a Make some chocolate eggs.

    b Take part in an egg-rolling race.

    c Decorate their own eggs.

    d Join an egg hunt.

( ) **2.** Where did the woman get information about the activity?

    a A book.

    b The Internet.

    c A friend.

    d A flyer.

( ) **3.** Which of these items is the man going to buy at the store?

    a Olive oil.

    b Chocolate eggs.

    c Jelly beans.

    d Marshmallows.

Tomb Sweeping Day
清明節

I Reading

19

Tomb Sweeping Day is a very important holiday for the Taiwanese. It's a day dedicated to worshipping and paying respect to the dead. It is also a national holiday, and most people are given the day off work so they can visit the **graves**[1] of their **ancestors**[2] to clean and care for the tombs. Graves are swept, and any weeds covering the tomb **removed**.[3] **Offerings**[4] of food are then placed **in front of** the grave, and **incense**[5] and **spirit money** are burned. Some people also burn paper models of **material**[6] goods such as cars or smartphones so their ancestors have the use of these things in the spirit world.

The origins of Tomb Sweeping Day go back to the 7th century BC and concern a **loyal**[7] court official named Jie Zitui, who served Duke Wen of Jin. Once, during a long period of **exile**[8] and hardship, Jie made soup for the duke using **flesh**[9] from his own leg when meat was **scarce**.[10] The duke promised to **reward**[11] Jie when he regained his kingdom, but when this finally happened, the duke forgot. After many years, the duke remembered his promise and, feeling **guilty**,[12] decided to find Jie in order to reward him.

▲ incense   ▲ spirit money

1. **grave** [grev] (n.) 墓穴
2. **ancestor** [ˈænsɛstɚ] (n.) 祖先
3. **remove** [rɪˈmuv] (v.) 去除
4. **offering** [ˈɔfərɪŋ] (n.) 供物，祭品
5. **incense** [ˈɪnsɛns] (n.) 香
6. **material** [məˈtɪrɪəl] (a.) 物質的
7. **loyal** [ˈlɔɪəl] (a.) 忠誠的
8. **exile** [ˈɛksaɪl] (n.) 流亡；放逐
9. **flesh** [flɛʃ] (n.) 肌肉；肉體

10. **scarce** [skɛrs] (a.) 缺乏的；稀有的
11. **reward** [rɪˈwɔrd] (v.) 報答；獎賞
12. **guilty** [ˈgɪltɪ] (a.) 內疚的

★ **spirit money** [ˈspɪrɪt ˈmʌnɪ] (n.) 紙錢

phr. **in front of** 在……之前

清明節對台灣人而言是個非常重要的節日，人們在這天會祭拜並追思亡者。清明節也是國定假日，大多數人都能放一天假，這樣才能回到祖先墳前打掃並整理他們的墓。人們會清掃並除掉遮掩墳墓的雜草，接著會在墳前放上貢品、點香並燒紙錢，有些人也會燒紙糊的實物模型，例如汽車或智慧型手機，供祖先在冥界使用。

清明節的起源可追溯自西元前七世紀，與一位名為介子推並侍奉晉文公的忠臣有關。在一次長期流亡與困境中，由於肉食難尋，介子推割下自己的大腿肉並煮湯給晉文公喝。晉文公發誓在奪回王國政權時會犒賞介子推，但當晉文公重掌政權時他卻忘了當時的應允。多年後，晉文公記起當時的誓言而心生愧疚，他決定尋找介子推並犒賞他。

▲ offerings

But Jie had gone to live deep in a mountain forest with his mother. The forest was **dense**,[13] and the duke was unable to find Jie. So it was suggested that he set fire to the forest to force Jie to come out. Tragically, Jie **perished**[14] in the fire, and the duke never got to thank him. Instead, he created a three-day ban on fire to be observed each year to commemorate his loyal friend. This was known as the Cold Food Festival. The emperor **decreed**[15] that the day after the Cold Food Festival should be devoted to honoring all the dead. And over time, the two festivals and their traditions **merged into** one—the Tomb Sweeping Day of today.

▼ dense

13. **dense** [dɛns] (a.) 濃密的
14. **perish** [ˈpɛrɪʃ] (v.) 死去
15. **decree** [dɪˈkri] (v.) 頒布法令

phr. **merge into** 合成；融合

decree ▶

　　然而介子推早已與母親隱居深山，山林茂密使晉文公遍尋不見介子推。有人建議晉文公放火燒山以逼出介子推，但悲劇發生了，介子因而死於火災，而晉文公永遠無法向他致上感激之意。有鑑於此，為了紀念他忠心的朋友，晉文公規定人們每年不得開火三天，這個節日被稱為寒食節。後來皇帝下令使寒食節後一日成為紀念所有亡者的日子，久而久之兩個節日和其傳統則合而為一，成為現今的清明節。

Ⅱ Reading Comprehension Questions

( ) **1.** When did Tomb Sweeping Day originate?
  a In the 7th century AD.
  b During the last century.
  c More than 2500 years ago.
  d In 2500 AD.

( ) **2.** What do people NOT do on Tomb Sweeping Day?
  a Get the day off work.
  b Clean their ancestors' tombs.
  c Burn spirit money.
  d Set off fireworks.

( ) **3.** Jie Zitui made soup for his master using which ingredient?
  a His own flesh.
  b Magic beans.
  c Powdered gold.
  d The flesh of a mythical animal.

( ) **4.** What did Duke Wen of Jin do to honor his friend Jie Zitui?
  a He burned down a forest.
  b He banned fire for three days each year.
  c He went to live in the mountains.
  d He made soup the national dish of China.

( ) **5.** What does it mean if something is "scarce"?
  a Only a small amount is available.
  b There's plenty of it available.
  c It tastes delicious.
  d It will stay fresh for a long time.

MAKING SPRING ROLLS

Xiao Yu It's almost dinner time. I should start making the spring rolls. Would you like to help me, Jack?

Jack Sure. I love spring rolls. I love how **crispy**[1] they are.

Xiao Yu You're thinking of fried spring rolls; the spring rolls we eat on Tomb Sweeping Day are a little different.

Jack Different? How?

Xiao Yu Well, first of all, we don't **fry**[2] them, so they're soft and **chewy**.[3] Second of all, they're much bigger.

Jack Interesting. So what do we do first?

Xiao Yu First we take the **flatbread**; then we add the **ingredients**[4] and **wrap** them **up**.

Jack That's pretty simple. I see we've got some vegetables, some meat, some **scrambled eggs** . . . We just throw them all in?

Xiao Yu That's right! You can season them with a little peanut **powder**[5] at the end if you like.

◀ flatbread

▲ scrambled eggs

◀ spring rolls

1. **crispy** [ˈkrɪspɪ] (a.) 酥脆的
2. **fry** [fraɪ] (v.) 煎；炸
3. **chewy** [ˈtʃuɪ] (a.) 有嚼勁的
4. **ingredient** [ɪnˈɡridɪənt] (n.)（烹飪的）原料
5. **powder** [ˈpaʊdɚ] (n.) 粉末

★ **flatbread** [ˈflætbrɛd] (n.) 薄餅
★ **scrambled eggs** [ˈskræmbl̩d ɛgs] (n.) 炒蛋

phr. **wrap up** 包起來；捲起來

46

做潤餅（春捲）

小玉：晚餐時間快到了，我得開始做春捲，傑克，你想幫我嗎？

傑克：好啊，我好喜歡春捲，我喜歡它酥脆的口感。

小玉：你想的是炸春捲，我們在清明節吃的春捲跟那個有點不同。

傑克：不同？如何不同？

小玉：嗯，首先，我們不會用炸的，所以它們軟嫩有嚼勁，第二，它們體積大很多。

傑克：真有趣，那麼我們該怎麼做？

小玉：首先，我們要拿餅皮，接著我們要把食材放在裡面然後把它們捲起來。

傑克：挺簡單的，我看到我們有一些蔬菜、肉類、炒蛋……我們都要把這些放進去嗎？

小玉：沒錯，然後若你喜歡的話，你最後可以用一些花生粉調味。

 **Listening Practice** **21**

( ) **1.** The speakers are most likely planning a trip to which of these places?

[a] The cemetery.

[b] The bank.

[c] The beach.

[d] The race track.

( ) **2.** Which of these items is the woman NOT going to buy?

[a] Fresh fruit.

[b] Flowers.

[c] Ghost money.

[d] A broom.

( ) **3.** Which of these statements is TRUE?

[a] The man wants to buy a new car.

[b] The man's father has passed away.

[c] The man does not own a weed remover.

[d] The man keeps his tools in the trunk of his car.

Mother's Day
母親節

I Reading

22

Do you know on which day of the year telephone lines in the United States **record**[1] the highest **traffic**[2]? You guessed it! On Mother's Day.

Sons and daughters who live far away from home use this day to **pick up** the phone and express their appreciation to the women who **raised**[3] them. Those who live with or near their mothers also show their **gratitude**,[4] perhaps by preparing breakfast in bed for their mothers or by taking them out for an expensive meal. Flowers, especially **carnations**, and cards are often presented as well.

The earliest observance of "Mother's Day" can be **traced back** to the ancient Greeks, who honored Rhea, the mother goddess of all **deities**, during the springtime. Starting in the 1600s in Europe, mothers were honored each year on the fourth Sunday in Lent, known as "Mothering Sunday."

However, the holiday celebrated today in the United States has much more recent roots and is largely attributed to the work of one woman, Ms. Anna Jarvis. Ms. Jarvis's mother was an **extraordinary**[5] woman. She was the mother of 11 children and was also an **activist**[6] during the American Civil War. Ms. Jarvis loved her mother dearly. When she died on May 10, 1905, Ms. Jarvis was **devastated**[7] and **vowed**[8] to dedicate her life to honoring her mother.

 raising a baby ▶

1. **record** [rɪ`kɔrd] (v.) 記載;記錄
2. **traffic** [`træfɪk] (n.) 運載量
3. **raise** [rez] (v.) 養育
4. **gratitude** [`grætə,tjud] (n.) 感激之情;感恩
5. **extraordinary** [ɪk`strɔrdn,ɛrɪ] (a.) 非凡的
6. **activist** [`æktəvɪst] (n.) 行動主義者
7. **devastated** [`dɛvəs,tetɪd] (a.) 身心交瘁的
8. **vow** [vau] (v.) 發誓

★ **carnation** [kɑr`neʃən] (n.) 康乃馨
★ **deity** [`diətɪ] (n.) 神

phr. **pick up** 拿起;拾起
phr. **trace back** 追溯自

carnations ▶

你知道美國每年哪天的電話通訊量會創下年度紀錄嗎?你猜對了!就是母親節。

離家遙遠的兒女在這天中會拿起電話,向養育他們的母親表達感激之意。而與母親同住或離家較近的兒女,則可能藉由準備讓母親可在床上享用的早餐,或帶母親出去吃頓大餐,致上感謝之意。兒女們也會給母親鮮花,特別是康乃馨,還有母親節卡片。

最早的母親節可追溯至古希臘人,他們在春日時分會祭拜「眾神之母」瑞亞。除此之外,歐洲從 17 世紀時在大齋期的第四個週日表揚母親,稱之為母親節(Mothering Sunday)。

然而,今日美國慶祝的母親節的主要幕後推手是安娜‧賈維斯女士,賈維斯女士的母親是位傑出女性,她育有 11 名子女且在美國內戰時是一位倡議分子。賈維斯女士十分深愛她的母親,當她母親於 1905 年五月十日逝世時,她大受打擊,並誓言要將她的生命致力於榮耀母親。

In 1908, Ms. Jarvis held a celebration for mothers in her local church. She gave white carnations to the **parishioners** who attended the celebration because those were her mother's favorite flower. In the following years, she started a large letter-writing campaign[9] to establish[10] an official[11] holiday for all mothers. In 1910, the **governor** of West Virginia declared the second Sunday in May a state holiday and named it Mother's Day. Many other states followed suit, and in 1914, President Woodrow Wilson officially made Mother's Day a national holiday.

9. **campaign** [kæmˋpen] (n.) 宣傳活動
10. **establish** [əˋstæblɪʃ] (v.) 建立
11. **official** [əˋfɪʃəl] (a.) 官方的

★ **parishioner** [pəˋrɪʃənɚ] (n.) 教區居民
★ **governor** [ˋgʌvənɚ] (n.) 州長

◀ governor

1908 年時，賈維斯女士在當地教會籌辦一場專為母親舉辦的慶祝活動，她給蒞臨的會眾白康乃馨，因為這是她母親生前最愛的花。爾後幾年，她開啟一場大型的寫信請願活動，希望能建立一個給所有母親的正式節日。1910 年時，西維吉尼亞的州長宣布五月的第二個星期日為州立節日，並命名為「母親節」。許多其他州紛紛仿效，到 1914 年時，伍德羅·威爾遜總統正式將母親節立為國定節慶。

II Reading Comprehension Questions

(   ) **1.** According to the passage, which of the following is NOT a
common Mother's Day gift?
  - a A meal at a restaurant.
  - b Breakfast in bed.
  - c Flowers.
  - d An envelope full of money.

(   ) **2.** Who was Ms. Jarvis's mother?
  - a A Civil War activist.
  - b A politician.
  - c A florist.
  - d A church leader.

(   ) **3.** How did Ms. Jarvis convince government
authorities to establish a holiday for all mothers?
  - a By growing carnations.
  - b By writing letters.
  - c By giving speeches.
  - d By painting pictures.

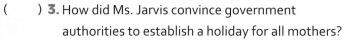

(   ) **4.** What US state was the first to establish Mother's Day as an
official holiday?
  - a Georgia.
  - b Florida.
  - c West Virginia.
  - d California.

(   ) **5.** In which year did Mother's Day become a national holiday in
the United States?
  - a 1914
  - b 1908
  - c 1910
  - d 1600

ⓘ Conversation

23

BUYING A MOTHER'S DAY GIFT

Jessie Mike, we need to talk about what to get Mom for Mother's Day.

Mike Well, a card **obviously**.[1] And I was thinking maybe we could get her **a bunch of** carnations.

Jessie Yeah, but we get her that every year. How about we get her a different gift this year?

Mike I don't mind getting her something else, but I think we should still get carnations because, you know, it's a tradition.

Jessie Well, I was thinking of getting her a nice **scarf**.[2] I saw a really beautiful **cashmere** one that I think she'll love.

Mike All right. I'll get the card and the flowers, and you pick up the scarf. We can **figure out** the **total**[3] **amount**[4] and **split**[5] it later.

Jessie Sounds good to me.

▼ a bunch of carnations

scarf ▶

1. **obviously** [ˈɑbvɪəslɪ] (adv.) 顯然地
2. **scarf** [skɑrf] (n.) 圍巾
3. **total** [ˈtotl̩] (a.) 總計的
4. **amount** [əˈmaʊnt] (n.) 總額
5. **split** [splɪt] (v.) 分攤

★ **cashmere** [ˈkæʃmɪr] (n.) 羊毛絨

phr. **a bunch of** 一束；一串；很多
phr. **figure out** 算清楚；了解

52

購買母親節禮物

潔西：麥克，我們得討論母親節禮物要買什麼。

麥克：嗯，卡片是一定要的，我在想也許我們可以送她一束康乃馨。

潔西：好啊，但我們每年都送她這個，我們今年送她不同的禮物如何？

麥克：我不介意送她不同的禮物，但我還是覺得我們應該要送她康乃馨，因為妳知道的，這是傳統。

潔西：好，那麼我想我們可以送她不錯的圍巾，我之前有看到一條很美的羊毛圍巾，我想她應該會很喜歡。

麥克：好啊，那我負責準備卡片和花，妳去買圍巾，我們之後看總共花了多少錢再一起分。

潔西：聽起來還不錯。

Ⅳ Listening Practice 🎧 24

(　　) **1.** What are the speakers talking about?
- a Taking their mother out for dinner.
- b What gift to buy their mother.
- c Their mother's favorite flower.
- d What they love about their mother.

(　　) **2.** During the conversation, what does the man give the woman?
- a A bunch of flowers.
- b A Mother's Day card.
- c A business card.
- d A menu.

(　　) **3.** Who is Johnny?
- a The speakers' teacher.
- b The speakers' uncle.
- c The speakers' cousin.
- d The speakers' brother.

Dragon Boat Festival

端午節

I Reading

25

Many Western holidays are celebrated to honor saints or other religious **figures**.[1] Few if any are held to commemorate **poets**.[2] The Dragon Boat Festival, celebrated on the fifth day of the fifth lunar month, is held each year in China, Taiwan, Singapore, and Malaysia to honor the poet and **statesman** Qu Yuan.

Qu Yuan lived over two thousand years ago during China's Warring States Period. He was a **supporter**[3] of the Chu kingdom and served it faithfully for many years. However, **corrupt**[4] **ministers**,[5] jealous of Qu, turned the king against him, and Qu was **banished**[6] from his home. During his exile, Qu Yuan wrote many famous poems expressing his

love for his country. Many years later, the capital of the Chu kingdom was **captured**[7] by the **armies**[8] of its great **rival**,[9] the Qin kingdom. In **despair**,[10] Qu Yuan **waded**[11] into the Milo River and drowned himself. The local villagers, who greatly admired the poet, raced out in their boats to try and save him. However, they were too late. To make sure that the fish would not eat his body, they threw balls of sticky rice into the water.

▲ wade

1. **figure** [ˈfɪgjɚ] (n.) 人物
2. **poet** [ˈpoɪt] (n.) 詩人
3. **supporter** [səˈportɚ] (n.) 支持者
4. **corrupt** [kəˈrʌpt] (a.) 貪污的;墮落的
5. **minister** [ˈmɪnɪstɚ] (n.) 部長;大臣
6. **banish** [ˈbænɪʃ] (v.) 流放
7. **capture** [ˈkæptʃɚ] (v.) 捕獲;俘虜
8. **army** [ˈɑrmɪ] (n.) 軍隊
9. **rival** [ˈraɪvl] (n.) 競爭者;敵人

10. **despair** [dɪˈspɛr] (n.) 絕望
11. **wade** [wed] (v.) 涉水

★ **statesman** [ˈstetsmən] (n.) 政治家

▲ sticky rice

屈原

▲ Qu Yuan

許多西方節日是為了紀念聖人或宗教人物而舉辦,就算有的話,很少節日是用來紀念詩人的。端午節在農曆五月五日舉行,每年在中國、台灣、新加坡和馬來西亞舉辦,紀念詩人兼政治家屈原。

屈原生於兩千年前,是中國的戰國時期。他效忠楚國,並忠心侍奉楚國多年,然而貪腐的朝廷官員因忌妒屈原,使楚王與他對立並將他趕出故鄉。在流放期間,屈原寫了許多知名詩詞表達愛國之意。多年後,楚國都城被該國的頭號敵人秦國攻下,在絕望之中,屈原投汩羅江而亡。十分愛戴這位詩人的當地居民,急駛船隻試圖救他,但卻為時已晚,為了不讓魚隻以他的屍體為食,他們將糯米製成的米糰投入河中。

In remembrance of the villagers' actions, every year people **take part in** dragon boat races on local rivers and lakes and also eat *zongzi*—sticky rice dumplings made with glutinous rice, meat, and **mushrooms** wrapped in bamboo leaves. Taiwan's annual[12] dragon boat races have become popular internationally, and teams from all over the world flock to the island to take part. Another Dragon Boat Festival tradition is the wearing of perfumed **pouches**. These colorful pouches **are filled with** a fragrant[13] powder made from Chinese herbs and are worn by children to **drive away** evil[14] spirits. This custom probably began because diseases and plagues[15] were common during the midsummer months. Nowadays, however, they are worn simply for decoration.

▲ dragon boat race

12. **annual** [ˈænjʊəl] (a.) 每年的
13. **fragrant** [ˈfreɡrənt] (a.) 香的；芳香的
14. **evil** [ˈivl̩] (a.) 邪惡的
15. **plague** [pleɡ] (n.) 瘟疫

★ **mushroom** [ˈmʌʃrum] (n.) 蘑菇；菇

★ **pouch** [paʊtʃ] (n.) 小袋；囊

phr. **take part in** 參加
phr. **be filled with** 被……裝滿
phr. **drive away** 趕走

為了感念當地居民的行為，人們每年都在當地河川或湖泊舉行龍舟比賽，也會吃粽子（糯米飯糰）——一種將糯米、肉和香菇包進粽葉的食物。台灣每年的龍舟比賽舉世聞名，世界各國的隊伍皆前往這個小島以參加比賽。端午節的另一項傳統是戴掛香包，這些五顏六色的香包中裝滿著由中藥所製成的香料粉，孩童掛在身上以驅魔避邪。相傳此習俗的起源是由於炎炎夏日中常有許多疾病和瘟疫盛行，但現今掛戴香包只是用來裝飾而已。

▶ zongzi

▲ perfumed pouch

Ⅱ Reading Comprehension Questions

( ) **1.** Who does Dragon Boat Festival honor?
  a A sailor.
  b A poet.
  c A saint.
  d A warrior.

( ) **2.** How did Qu Yuan die?
  a He was murdered.
  b He died of an illness.
  c He killed himself.
  d He died of old age.

( ) **3.** How did the local people feel about Qu Yuan?
  a They loved him.
  b They feared him.
  c They hated him.
  d They envied him.

( ) **4.** What was the original reason for wearing pouches filled with herbs on Dragon Boat Festival?
  a To attract members of the opposite sex.
  b To bring good luck.
  c To prevent diseases.
  d To get rid of the smell of *zongzi*.

( ) **5.** Which of the following is TRUE about dragon boat races?
  a Foreigners are allowed to participate.
  b They happen once every two years.
  c They're held in swimming pools.
  d They're thought to drive away evil spirits.

PREPARING ZONGZI

Xiao Ming OK, Grandma. Tell me what I need to do.

Grandma First **soak**¹ the **sticky rice** in water.

Xiao Ming How much rice do we need?

Grandma About five **bowls**² of rice, and five bowls of water.

▲ dried shrimp

Xiao Ming OK. What next?

Grandma Now I need you to **chop**³ the pork belly into chunks, put them in a bowl, and cover them with **soy sauce**.

Xiao Ming Is that to give the meat more flavor?

Grandma Yes. While you're doing that, I'll start soaking the dried mushrooms, the peanuts, and the dried **shrimp**.⁴

Xiao Ming What do I do after I'm done with the pork?

Grandma Go and get the **bamboo**⁵ leaves and soak them in water, too. We want them to be nice and soft.

Xiao Ming So they don't break when we're wrapping the ingredients, right?

Grandma That's right. Now we just need to wait for a few hours until everything's ready.

◀ bamboo leaves

1. **soak** [sok] (v.) 浸泡
2. **bowl** [bol] (n.) 碗
3. **chop** [tʃɑp] (v.) 剁；切
4. **shrimp** [ʃrɪmp] (n.) 蝦
5. **bamboo** [bæmˈbu] (n.) 竹

★ **sticky rice** [ˈstɪkɪ raɪs] (n.) 糯米
★ **soy sauce** [sɔɪ sɔs] (n.) 醬油

▲ mushrooms

▲ soy sauce

準備包粽子

小明：好的，奶奶，告訴我該怎麼做。
奶奶：先把糯米浸泡在水中。
小明：我們需要多少米呢？
奶奶：大概五碗米和五碗水。
小明：好，接下來呢？
奶奶：現在我需要你把豬肚切塊，放到碗裡，並用醬油醃製。
小明：這是要讓肉更有味道對吧？
奶奶：是啊，當你這麼做時，我會泡乾香菇、花生和蝦米。
小明：那麼等我醃好肉時我要做什麼？
奶奶：去拿竹葉並也將它們浸在水中，我們需要乾淨又軟的竹葉。
小明：這樣竹葉才不會在我們包食材時破掉對吧？
奶奶：沒錯，現在我們需要等幾個小時讓一切就緒。

IV Listening Practice 🎧 27

(　　) **1.** Who are the speakers?

    [a] Olympic rowers.

    [b] Students.

    [c] Musicians.

    [d] Chefs.

(　　) **2.** Which of the following is TRUE about the female speaker?

    [a] She used to row for England.

    [b] She competed in a dragon boat race last year.

    [c] She has never rowed before.

    [d] She is not interested in competing this year.

(　　) **3.** How many people are needed to form a team?

    [a] 10

    [b] 15

    [c] 22

    [d] 20

Independence Day
美國獨立紀念日

I Reading

28

   Independence Day, also known as the Fourth of July, is arguably the day on which Americans are at their most **patriotic**.[1] It's a celebration that marks the birth of the United States on July 4, 1776, when the 13 British **colonies**[2] on the North American **continent**[3] **declared**[4] themselves an independent nation.

   In the years leading up to 1776, the two and a half million people living in Britain's American colonies were becoming increasingly **discontent**[5] with their rulers back in England. The colonists felt it **unjust**[6] that they were asked to pay **taxes**[7] to England when the British Crown did not allow them **elected**[8] **representation**[9] in the British

Parliament. A popular saying at that time was "no taxation without representation." Then, after more than 10 years of **protest**[10] and struggle, the colonists decided to seek **independence**[11] from their mother nation.

In June 1776, a **committee**[12] was **formed**,[13] and **the head of** the committee, Thomas Jefferson, **drafted**[14] the famous Declaration of Independence, which later became the symbol of the holiday.

▲ elect　　　▲ protest

1. **patriotic** [ˌpetrɪˈɑtɪk] (a.) 愛國的
2. **colony** [ˈkɑlənɪ] (n.) 殖民地
3. **continent** [ˈkɑntənənt] (n.) 大陸；大洲
4. **declare** [dɪˈklɛr] (v.) 宣布；宣告
5. **discontent** [ˌdɪskənˈtɛnt] (a.) 不滿的
6. **unjust** [ʌnˈdʒʌst] (a.) 不公平的
7. **tax** [tæks] (n.) 稅
8. **elect** [ɪˈlɛkt] (v.) 選舉
9. **representation** [ˌrɛprɪzɛnˈteʃən] (n.) 代表

10. **protest** [ˈprotɛst] (n.) 抗議
11. **independence** [ˌɪndɪˈpɛndəns] (n.) 獨立
12. **committee** [kəˈmɪtɪ] (n.) 委員會
13. **form** [fɔrm] (v.) 成立；構成
14. **draft** [dræft] (v.) 起草

phr. **the head of** ……的領導人

▲ American Revolution

美國獨立紀念日，也稱為七月四日國慶日，被認為是美國人最能展現愛國情懷的一天。這個節日慶祝美國於 1776 年七月四日誕生，當時北美大陸共有 13 個英屬殖民地宣布他們將成為一個獨立的國度。

在 1776 前幾年，共有 250 萬人住在北美的英屬殖民地，並對英國的統治越來越不滿。這些被殖民者感到不平，因為他們被要求繳稅給英國，且英國皇室不允許他們在英國議會中選出代表，而當時的盛行口號是：「無代表，不納稅。」經過十年的抗議和努力，這些被殖民者決定要脫離母國統治並獨立。

1776 年的六月，五人小組成立，並由小組領導者湯瑪斯‧傑佛遜起草知名的美國獨立宣言，此後成為本節日的象徵。

The draft was presented to **Congress** on June 28. After several revisions,[15] the document declaring independence was signed on July 4, 1776. Though it took seven further years for the United States to defeat[16] England and attain[17] true freedom from British rule, July 4—the day on which the Declaration of Independence was signed—is seen as the birthday of the United States.

▲ Thomas Jefferson

▲ Star-Spangled Banner

Independence Day is now a holiday marked by parades and marching bands. Shops are decorated in red, white, and blue, the three colors that **make up** the Star-Spangled Banner. Baseball dominates[18] the TV schedules, and people go on picnics, have barbecues in their backyards, and watch something they **can't afford to** miss in the evening—the fireworks.

15. **revision** [rɪˈvɪʒən] (n.) 修訂
16. **defeat** [dɪˈfit] (v.) 戰勝；擊敗
17. **attain** [əˈten] (v.) 達到
18. **dominate** [ˈdɑməˌnet] (v.) 支配；控制

★ **Congress** [ˈkɑŋgrəs] (n.) 美國國會

phr. **make up** 組成
phr. **can't afford to** 不能冒……的險

▲ signing of the Declaration of Independence

此宣言於六月 28 日呈給美國國會，經過多次修訂後，獨立宣言於 1776 年七月四日簽訂。雖然美國在七年之後才打敗英國，真正脫離英國統治取得真正的自由，但宣言簽訂的七月四日被認為是美國的生日。

美國獨立紀念日現在以遊行和軍樂隊而聞名，商店皆由紅、白、藍三色做裝飾，因為這是美國國旗的三原色。這天中，電視節目以棒球比賽為主，人們會出外野餐，在後院烤肉，並在晚上欣賞絕不能錯過的節目——煙火。

II Reading Comprehension Questions

( ) **1.** Before 1776, how many colonies did the British have in America?
   a 13
   b 14
   c 15
   d 16

( ) **2.** What were the colonists NOT allowed to do?
   a Travel to England.
   b Elect their own Members of Parliament.
   c Pay taxes.
   d Get an education.

( ) **3.** What did Thomas Jefferson write the first draft of in June, 1776?
   a The Statement of Freedom.
   b The Declaration of Independence.
   c The Announcement of Liberty.
   d The Bulletin of Individuality.

( ) **4.** What is "the Star-Spangled Banner" most likely another name for?
   a The American flag.
   b The 13 British colonies.
   c Thomas Jefferson.
   d Congress.

( ) **5.** Which of the following does Independence Day celebrate?
   a America's victory over the British.
   b American sport.
   c America's birthday.
   d America's British heritage.

▲ fireworks

29

(▮▮▮) Conversation

BOOKING A HOTEL TO SEE FIREWORKS

Reception   Inter City Hotel, this is Richard. How may I help you?

Kim   Hello, I'd like to **book**[1] a room for the third and fourth of July.

Reception   I'm terribly sorry, but we're all booked up for the Fourth of July weekend.

Kim   Oh dear. My husband and I were hoping to visit New York to see the Fourth of July **fireworks**.[2] Do you know anywhere else that might have a room available?

Reception   Hmm . . . I think it's going to be very difficult for you to find a room for those dates. Everyone wants to be in New York that weekend to see the show.

Kim   OK. Well, thanks for your help. I'll try a few more hotels anyway. Maybe we'll get lucky.

Reception   All right. Thank you for calling. And Good luck!

1. **book** [bʊk] (v.) 預訂
2. **firework** [ˋfaɪr͵wɝk] (n.) 煙火

訂飯店看煙火

飯店櫃檯：市際飯店，我是李察，有什麼需要我服務的地方嗎？

小金：哈囉，我想要預訂七月三日和四日的房間。

飯店櫃檯：我深感遺憾，但國慶日週末的房間都已客滿了。

小金：喔天啊，我先生和我想去紐約看國慶日煙火，您知道哪裡可能還有空房嗎？

飯店櫃檯：嗯……要在那幾天為您找到空房實在很困難，大家都想在那週末來紐約看煙火。

小金：好吧，感謝您的幫忙，我還是會再多試幾間飯店，也許我們會幸運找到。

飯店櫃檯：好的，感謝您的來電，祝您好運。

IV Listening Practice

30

(　　) **1.** What is the man going to film the woman doing?

    a Reading a patriotic poem.

    b Singing the national anthem.

    c Dancing to the national anthem.

    d Reading the Declaration of Independence.

(　　) **2.** What's the prize for the winner?

    a The chance to perform at a special event.

    b A letter of congratulations from the President.

    c A contract with a record company.

    d An article written about him or her in the paper.

(　　) **3.** Who will judge the contest?

    a The mayor.

    b The editor of the newspaper.

    c The public.

    d A local celebrity.

Father's Day
父親節

I Reading

31

Seeing as there is Mother's Day to honor the world's mothers, it's only fair that there should also be Father's Day—a day to honor the world's fathers. This was the **exact**[1] reasoning that **motivated**[2] Sonora Louise Smart Dodd of Spokane, Washington to begin her campaign for a nationally **recognized**[3] Father's Day.

The idea came to her in 1909 while listening to a sermon at her local church about Anna Jarvis's creation of Mother's Day. Dodd was greatly **inspired**[4] by Jarvis's **efforts**[5] to make Mother's Day a national holiday and completely understood Jarvis's **devotion**[6] to her beloved parent. Dodd's own father, a Civil War **veteran**, was **widowed**[7] when his wife died in **childbirth**.[8] He had made countless **sacrifices**[9] and shown unconditional love in raising her and her five **siblings**.[10] Therefore, to commemorate her father, she convinced the Spokane Ministerial Association to support the idea of holding a special Father's Day celebration.

Although Dodd **initially**[11] chose June 5, her father's birthday, for the celebration, she failed to provide event **organizers**[12] enough time to make arrangements, and **consequently**[13] the first Father's Day observance was **postponed**[14] to June 19, 1910, the third Sunday of that month.

Father's Day greeting card ▶

1. **exact** [ɪgˋzækt] (a.) 準確的
2. **motivate** [ˋmotə,vet] (v.) 激勵
3. **recognize** [ˋrɛkəg,naɪz] (v.) 被認可
4. **inspire** [ɪnˋspaɪr] (v.) 鼓舞；激勵
5. **effort** [ˋɛfət] (n.) 努力
6. **devotion** [dɪˋvoʃən] (n.) 奉獻；摯愛
7. **widow** [ˋwɪdo] (v.) 使成寡婦／鰥夫
8. **childbirth** [ˋtʃaɪld,bɝθ] (n.) 生產
9. **sacrifice** [ˋsækrə,faɪs] (n.) 犧牲
10. **sibling** [ˋsɪblɪŋ] (n.) 手足
11. **initially** [ɪˋnɪʃəlɪ] (adv.) 最初地
12. **organizer** [ˋɔrgə,naɪzɚ] (n.) 籌備者
13. **consequently** [ˋkɑnsə,kwɛntlɪ] (adv.) 結果
14. **postpone** [postˋpon] (v.) 延期

★ **veteran** [ˋvɛtərən] (n.) 老兵；榮民

　　既然有母親節以感謝全天下的母親，總該也有父親節以表彰全天下的父親以示公平。這正是住在美國華盛頓州斯波坎的杜德夫人（索諾拉‧露易絲‧史馬特‧杜德）的想法，她因此開啟爭取成立國定父親節的活動。

　　這個想法始於 1909 年，杜德夫人在當地教會聽到一則講道，內容關於安娜‧賈維斯女士所創立的母親節。杜德夫人深受賈維斯女士的啟發，她完全了解賈維斯女士推動母親節成為國定節日的努力，還有她對摯愛母親的全心奉獻。杜德夫人的父親是位美國內戰老兵，他因妻子難產去世而成為鰥夫，他在養育杜德夫人和她的其他五位手足時，做出無數的犧牲奉獻並展現出無私的愛。因此，為了紀念她的父親，她說服斯波坎牧者協會來支持她的想法，舉辦一場特別的父親節禮讚。

　　雖然杜德夫人原本選定在她父親的生日六月五日舉辦慶祝活動，她卻因沒給主辦單位足夠的活動籌辦時間，使得第一個父親節被延至 1910 年六月 19 日，是該月的第三個星期日。

▲ ◀ Sonora Louise Smart Dodd and her father

67

Since then, Father's Day has always fallen on the third Sunday in June in the United States. Many other countries now celebrate Father's Day, too, though not necessarily on the same date as in the United States. In Taiwan, for example, Father's Day is celebrated on August 8, as the date, when read aloud in Chinese, sounds like the word for "father."

Nowadays,[15] Father's Day is celebrated much the same way as Mother's Day, by taking one's father out to dinner or sending greeting cards. Another practice that **mimics**[16] the Mother's Day tradition is the wearing and giving of flowers. While the carnation is the flower for Mother's Day, roses are associated with Father's Day. People give or wear red roses if their fathers are alive, while white roses are worn to honor one's father who has **passed away**.

15. **nowadays** [ˈnaʊəˌdez] (adv.) 時下;當今
16. **mimic** [ˈmɪmɪk] (v.) 模仿

phr. **pass away** 過世

從此之後,美國的父親節一直都定在六月的第三個星期日。現今也有許多其他的國家慶祝父親節,雖然日子不盡然跟美國相同,例如台灣的父親節是在八月八日慶祝,因為這個日期的中文讀音聽起來很像「爸爸」。

現在,慶祝父親節的方式跟母親節頗為相似,包括請父親吃頓晚餐或是贈送感恩卡片,另一項模仿母親節的傳統是配戴花朵或獻花。母親節的代表花是康乃馨,而父親節的代表花則是玫瑰。若一個人的父親仍然健在,會配戴或送紅玫瑰;而若父親已過世,則會配戴白玫瑰以表紀念。

II Reading Comprehension Questions

(　　) **1.** What gave Dodd the idea of establishing Father's Day?
  a She heard about Jarvis's efforts to promote Mother's Day.
  b Her father died during her childhood.
  c Her husband was a wonderful father.
  d She never knew her father.

(　　) **2.** How many children did Dodd's father have?
  a Five.
  b Six.
  c Seven.
  d Four.

(　　) **3.** When Father's Day was first being established, why was it set on the third Sunday in June?
  a It was the birthday of Dodd's father.
  b It was the anniversary of the end of the Civil War.
  c There wasn't enough time to prepare the event for another date.
  d The date sounds special when read aloud.

(　　) **4.** According to the passage, which of the following is NOT done to celebrate Father's Day?
  a People take their fathers out to a restaurant.
  b People give their fathers greeting cards.
  c People take their fathers to church.
  d People give their fathers flowers.

(　　) **5.** What color rose do you wear on Father's Day if your father is alive?
  a Pink.
  b White.
  c Red.
  d Black.

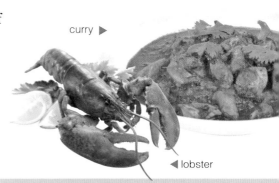
A FATHER'S DAY MEAL

Mom Jake, come here, quickly.

Jake What's up, Mom?

Mom While your father's in the shower, we need to decide where to take him for Father's Day.

Jake Right. How about that Indian restaurant Taj Mahal? You know how much Dad loves **curry**.[1]

Mom That's not a bad idea. But I was thinking of something perhaps a bit more **upscale**.[2] We can eat Indian any time.

Jake Umm, OK. What about The Seashell? It got some great **reviews**[3] in the local paper.

Mom The seafood restaurant on Fifth? Yeah, OK. Your father will love that.

Jake Yeah, especially if he can stuff himself with **lobster** and not have to pay for it himself!

curry ▶

Mom I'll give them a call and see if they've got a table. Hopefully they won't be full up!

◀ lobster

1. **curry** [ˋkɝɪ] (n.) 咖哩
2. **upscale** [ˋʌpˌskel] (a.) 高檔的
3. **review** [rɪˋvju] (n.) 評論

★ **lobster** [ˋlɑbstɚ] (n.) 龍蝦

upscale ▶

父親節大餐

媽媽：傑克，快過來。

傑克：媽，怎麼了嗎？

媽媽：趁你爸洗澡的時候，我們來決定父親節要帶他去哪裡吃飯。

傑克：對齁，那間印度餐廳「泰姬瑪陵」如何？你也知道爸很愛吃咖哩。

媽媽：這個主意還不賴，但我在想我們也許可以找更高檔的餐廳，畢竟我們隨時都可以吃印度菜。

傑克：嗯好，那麼「貝殼餐廳」如何？它在報紙上的評價很棒。

媽媽：第五大道上的那間海鮮餐廳嗎？好啊，你爸應該會很喜歡。

傑克：是啊，又特別是他可以大吃龍蝦而且還不用自己付錢。

媽媽：我來打電話給它們看看還有沒有位子，希望還沒客滿。

IV Listening Practice

( ) **1.** What is the woman doing?

    a Making a restaurant reservation.

    b Buying a cake.

    c Cooking a special meal.

    d Ordering takeout.

( ) **2.** Which of the following is the father's favorite dish?

    a Steak and fries.

    b Beef and onion soup.

    c Roast beef and potatoes.

    d Beef curry.

( ) **3.** When will the boy's father arrive home?

    a In two hours.

    b In one hour.

    c Tomorrow.

    d In 30 minutes.

Ghost Festival
中元節

I Reading

🎧 34

For Chinese people all over the world, the seventh month of the lunar calendar is known as Ghost Month. Similar to Halloween in the West, Ghost Month is a time when the **gates**[1] of hell are opened, and ghosts are free to **roam**[2] the earth.

Perhaps the most feared of these **spirits**[3] are the ghosts of those whose **descendants**[4] did not make offerings to them after they died. As a result, the ghosts have become stick thin, with long hanging limbs, pencil-necks, and large **swollen**[5] bellies that **torment**[6] them with **eternal**[7] hunger.

On the fifteenth day of Ghost Month, food is offered and incense and ghost money are burned to **appease**[8] these wandering spirits. In addition, **entertainment**[9] is provided for the ghosts in the form of traditional concerts and shows, such as Taiwanese opera or **glove puppetry**. To **make sure** the ghosts have the best seats, the front row of seats at these shows are deliberately left empty.

The origins of Ghost Month are unclear, but they are rooted in Buddhist, Taoist, and Confucian traditions. One story that is particularly popular tells of a talented Buddhist monk called Mulian, who discovered that his **deceased**[10] mother was being **punished**[11] in hell due to her greed and **spitefulness**[12] while still alive.

▼ gate

▲ food offerings　　　　▲ Buddha

1. **gate** [get] (n.) 大門
2. **roam** [rom] (v.) 漫遊；遊蕩
3. **spirit** [ˋspɪrɪt] (n.) 靈魂；鬼魂
4. **descendant** [dɪˋsɛndənt] (n.) 子孫；後裔
5. **swollen** [ˋswolən] (a.) 浮腫的
6. **torment** [ˋtɔr͵mɛnt] (v.) 使痛苦或苦惱
7. **eternal** [ɪˋtɝn!] (a.) 永恆的
8. **appease** [əˋpiz] (v.) 撫慰
9. **entertainment** [͵ɛntɚˋtenmənt] (n.) 餘興；娛樂
10. **deceased** [dɪˋsist] (a.) 已過世的

11. **punish** [ˋpʌnɪʃ] (v.) 懲罰
12. **spitefulness** [ˋspaɪtfəlnɪs] (n.) 惡毒

★ **glove puppetry** [glʌv ˋpʌpɪtrɪ] (n.) 布袋戲

phr. **make sure** 確保

◀ glove puppetry
(cc by Yi-rou Tsai)

對於全世界的華人而言，農曆七月又被稱為鬼月。它類似西方的萬聖節，在這段時間鬼門會開啟，而鬼魂能自由在陽間遊蕩。

也許最令人畏懼的鬼魂是那些死後未受子孫祭拜的魂魄，正因如此，他們骨瘦如柴，有著細長的四肢、纖細的脖子和腫脹的腹部，讓他們永遠飽受飢餓之苦。

鬼月的第 15 日，人們會供奉食物並上香，也會燒紙錢以普渡遊蕩的鬼魂。除此之外，人們也會提供鬼魂傳統戲曲類的娛樂節目，例如歌仔戲或布袋戲。為了確保鬼魂們能擁有最佳視野，還特地將觀眾席的第一排空出來。

鬼月的源起難考，但都源自佛教、道教或儒家傳統。不過，其中最廣為流傳的故事是跟一位佛教高僧目連有關，他發現他已故的母親因在世時貪得無厭，因此被罰在地獄中受苦。

▲ Taiwanese opera

Whenever he tried to use his powers to send her food, it would turn into fire on her lips. He asked Buddha how he could feed his mother, and Buddha taught him the **rituals**[13] that would allow his mother to eat and, later, be reborn into human form.

Because of the **potentially**[14] harmful nature of these ghosts, many people avoid certain activities during Ghost Month. Swimming, for example, is avoided for fear of being taken by the spirits of the **drowned**.[15] People also try not to move house during this time, because by moving into a new house they might **disturb**[16] any ghosts living there. Businessmen avoid making important business deals so that their success won't be **cursed**[17] by a spiteful spirit.

13. **ritual** [ˈrɪtʃuəl] (n.) 儀式
14. **potentially** [pəˈtɛnʃəlɪ] (adv.) 潛在地；可能地
15. **drown** [draʊn] (v.) 淹死；溺死
16. **disturb** [dɪsˈtɝb] (v.) 打擾；擾亂
17. **curse** [kɝs] (v.) 詛咒

◀ curse

每當目連試著用自己的法力送食物給母親時，食物到她嘴邊則化為火焰。他詢問佛祖要如何餵飽母親，而佛祖則教他一套能讓母親進食的儀式，之後再投胎轉世為人。

由於這些鬼魂本身帶有不利霉運，許多人在鬼月會避免從事某些活動。游泳就是其中一例，人們避免游泳因為怕被溺死鬼抓交替。人們也盡量避免在此時搬家，因為搬新家時可能會打擾住在那裡的陰靈。而生意人則會避免在此時進行重要的交易，這樣他們的成功才不會被惡靈詛咒。

Ⅱ Reading Comprehension Questions

(　　) **1.** Which of the following do wandering ghosts have, according to the article?

    [a] Thin necks.

    [b] Short arms and legs.

    [c] Long hair.

    [d] Flat stomachs.

(　　) **2.** What happened to the food that Mulian tried to send to his dead mother?

    [a] It was stolen by the demons of hell.

    [b] It burned up when she put it to her mouth.

    [c] It got lost on the way to hell.

    [d] It was taken away by Buddha.

(　　) **3.** What is true about the descendants of wandering ghosts according to the article?

    [a] They did not make offerings to their ancestors.

    [b] They committed many crimes.

    [c] They died of hunger.

    [d] They offended Buddha.

(　　) **4.** Which of the following activities is NOT avoided during Ghost Month?

    [a] Swimming.

    [b] Moving house.

    [c] Making an important business deal.

    [d] Putting on a concert.

(　　) **5.** When are food and ghost money offered to wandering ghosts?

    [a] The twentieth day of the eighth lunar month.

    [b] The fifteenth day of the seventh lunar month.

    [c] The seventh day of the twelfth lunar month.

    [d] The sixteenth day of the sixth lunar month.

DANCING ZHONG KUI

Chris My Chinese teacher mentioned something in class yesterday that I didn't understand.

Xiao Mei What was it? Maybe I can explain it to you.

Chris It was about Ghost Month, and she mentioned something called "dancing Zhong Kui."

Xiao Mei Well, in Chinese **legend**,[1] Zhong Kui is known as the Ghost Hunter. And "dancing Zhong Kui" refers to a kind of ritual performed by a Taoist **priest**.[2]

Chris Oh, so it's like an **exorcism**?

▲ Zhong Kui, the Ghost Hunter

Xiao Mei Something like that. At the end of Ghost Month, it's believed that some ghosts don't want to return to Hell.

Chris I get it. So this priest performs a ritual to **send** them **away**?

Xiao Mei Yes, but it's a very special ritual. The priest actually dresses up as Zhong Kui and dances around, acting like him.

Chris Oh, right. So the ghosts think that the Ghost Hunter has come to get them and they leave.

Xiao Mei Exactly.

◀ Taoist priest

1. **legend** [ˈlɛdʒənd] (n.) 傳說；傳奇故事
2. **priest** [prist] (n.) 神職人員

★ **exorcism** [ˈɛksɔrˌsɪzəm] (n.) 驅邪；驅鬼

phr. **send away** 趕走

跳鍾馗

克里斯：我的中文老師昨天在課堂中提到一件我不太懂的事。

曉　玫：是什麼？也許我可以解釋給你聽。

克里斯：是有關鬼月，她提到一個叫「跳鍾馗」的活動。

曉　玫：嗯，在中國傳說中，鍾馗是知名的驅邪之神，而「跳鍾馗」是指一種由道士進行的活動儀式。

克里斯：喔，所以這像是一種驅魔儀式嗎？

曉　玫：有點像，在鬼月的月底，人們相信有些鬼魂不願意回到陰間。

克里斯：我懂了，所以道士就進行某種儀式把鬼趕回去？

曉　玫：是啊，但這場儀式非常特別，道士會打扮成驅邪之神鍾馗的樣子，並學其舉止，邁步揮手。

克里斯：喔，是喔，所以鬼會認為鍾馗要來抓他們了，所以就離開了。

曉　玫：沒錯。

IV Listening Practice 🎧 36

(　　) **1.** What are the speakers preparing?

　　a Food offerings.

　　b Dinner.

　　c A picnic.

　　d A gift basket.

(　　) **2.** How many types of fruit have they prepared?

　　a Three.

　　b Six.

　　c Four.

　　d Ten.

(　　) **3.** What does the mother say about the chicken?

　　a It has to have three layers.

　　b It has to be cut in half.

　　c It has to be served on an odd number of plates.

　　d It has to be served whole.

Moon Festival
中秋節

Celebrated in the middle of autumn, on the fifteenth day of the eighth lunar month, The Moon Festival is one of Taiwan's most pleasurable festivals. It's a time for getting together with family, barbecuing on the roadside or in parks, eating moon cakes and **pomelos**, and appreciating the beauty of the large, bright **harvest moon**.

People celebrate Moon Festival to give thanks, which is a reason that is common to the celebration of many other autumn festivals around the world, with autumn being the traditional time for harvest.[1] The admiration of the full moon itself, however, is **linked to** the fact that in Chinese culture the full moon is a strong symbol of family unity[2] and reunion. The eating of pomelos, harvested during this time, is also connected to the moon since the pomelo's roundness is distinctly[3] moon-like. However, there is an additional reason for eating them: the Chinese word for "pomelo" is a **homophone** of "blessing."

Chang'e, the moon goddess ▶

The main myth connected with the Moon Festival is that of Chang'e, the moon goddess. However, there are many versions of her story. According to one of them, long ago, 10 suns suddenly appeared in the sky. An archer called Hou Yi shot down nine of these suns, thus **saving** the earth **from** being burned to a **cinder**. As a reward, he was given the **elixir**[4] of life. Some said that Hou Yi was made king after shooting down the suns, but he soon became **cruel**[5] and **ruthless**.[6]

1. **harvest** [ˈhɑrvɪst] (n.) 收穫；收成
2. **unity** [ˈjunətɪ] (n.) 團結
3. **distinctly** [dɪˈstɪŋktlɪ] (adv.) 清楚地
4. **elixir** [ɪˈlɪksə] (n.) 長生不老藥
5. **cruel** [ˈkruəl] (a.) 殘忍的
6. **ruthless** [ˈruθlɪs] (a.) 無情的

▲ pomelos

★ **homophone** [ˈhɑməˌfon] (n.) 異義同音字
★ **cinder** [ˈsɪndə] (n.) 煤渣，炭渣

★ **pomelo** [ˈpɑmələ] (n.) 柚子
★ **harvest moon** [ˈhɑrvɪst mun] (n.) 滿月

phr. **link to** 與……有關
phr. **save . . . from** 讓……免於

▲ harvest moon

中秋節在秋天中期農曆八月 15 日舉行，是台灣最歡樂的佳節之一。人們會在此時與家人團聚，在路邊或公園裡烤肉，品嚐月餅和柚子，並欣賞最大且最皎潔明亮的滿月。

人們慶祝中秋節是為了感恩，很多國家慶祝許多其他秋季節慶也是這個原因，因為秋季是收成的季節。不過賞月本身，則是與滿月在中國文化象徵家族團圓有關。而吃在秋季盛產的柚子也與月亮有關，柚子圓滾滾的形狀就像月亮一般。然而，吃柚子還有另一個原因：中文字柚子的「柚」與保佑的「佑」是同音字。

與中秋節有關的主要傳說是月神嫦娥的故事，不過其版本眾說紛紜。傳說很久以前，天上突然出現十個太陽，一位名為后羿的神射手射下九個太陽，讓大地免於被烤成焦炭。為了犒賞后羿，他得到長生不老的仙藥。有人相傳，后羿在射日後成為皇帝，但很快地變成暴虐不仁。

His wife, Chang'e, took the elixir herself in order to save the people from being ruled forever by a **tyrant**.[7] The moment she **swallowed**[8] the elixir, she **floated**[9] out of the window and up towards the sky, eventually landing on the moon. According to another version of the story, Hou Yi, not wanting to be **immortal**[10] without his wife, gave her the elixir to hold for safe keeping. However, while he was away, one of his **apprentices**[11] broke into his house and tried to **force**[12] Chang'e to hand over the elixir. **Rather than** giving it to him, Chang'e swallowed the elixir herself. In order to be close to her husband, she **settled**[13] on the moon—the nearest place to the earth from heaven.

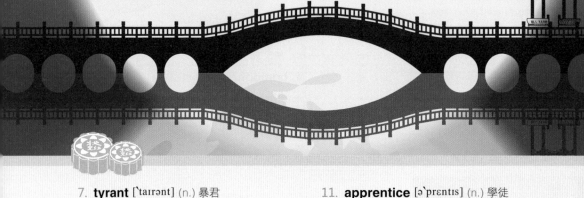

7. **tyrant** [ˈtaɪrənt] (n.) 暴君
8. **swallow** [ˈswɑlo] (v.) 吞；嚥
9. **float** [flot] (v.) 飄
10. **immortal** [ɪˈmɔrtl̩] (a.) 長生不老的

11. **apprentice** [əˈprɛntɪs] (n.) 學徒
12. **force** [fors] (v.) 迫使
13. **settle** [ˈsɛtl̩] (v.) 安頓；定居

phr. **rather than** 而不是……

他的妻子嫦娥喝了仙藥以免百姓永受暴君統治。她一喝下仙藥，飄出窗外並飛上天空，最終停在月亮。根據另一個版本，后羿不希望拋下妻子嫦娥獨自成仙，將仙藥給予嫦娥保管，然而后羿的學徒趁他離家之際闖入他家，並試著逼迫嫦娥交出仙藥。為了不讓他得逞，嫦娥自己服下藥水，為了能就近守候丈夫，她以月亮為居——是天庭中離人間最近的所在。

▲ moon cakes

II Reading Comprehension Questions

(   ) **1.** What is the full moon a symbol of in Taiwan?

     a A full belly.

     b Family unity.

     c Wealth.

     d Long life.

(   ) **2.** Which of the following is NOT a reason why pomelos are eaten during Moon Festival?

     a They're round like a full moon.

     b The word "pomelo" sounds like "blessing" in Chinese.

     c Pomelos are harvested around Moon Festival.

     d Pomelos were Chang'e's favorite fruit.

(   ) **3.** According to the first version of Chang'e's story, why did Chang'e swallow the elixir of life?

     a She wanted to live forever.

     b She wanted to punish her husband for treating her badly.

     c She mistook it for something else.

     d She wanted to protect the people from her husband.

(   ) **4.** Which of the following are people most likely to eat on Moon Festival?

     a Barbecued meat.

     b Freshly steamed bread.

     c Sticky rice cake.

     d Leftovers from the previous day.

(   ) **5.** According to the second version of Chang'e's story, why did Chang'e choose to live on the moon?

     a So she could be as close as possible to her husband.

     b So she could watch over and protect the earth.

     c So she could keep the elixir of life away from humanity.

     d So she could be left alone.

III Conversation

38

HAVING A BARBECUE

Lao Pang Gemma, do you have any plans for Moon Festival?

Gemma Not yet. Are you guys having a **barbecue**?[1]

Lao Pang Yes, we're going to the local park. You're welcome to join us.

Gemma Great. I'd love to. Shall I bring any food or drinks?

Lao Pang Just bring whatever you want to drink. For food, I'll just buy a bunch of stuff and we can all split the cost later.

Gemma OK. Hang on. When is Moon Festival? On Friday?

Lao Pang Yeah.

Gemma Do you know what the weather's going to be like? I remember last year all we got were clouds and rain. Will we be able to see the moon at least?

Lao Pang I checked the weather **forecast**.[2] Apparently, it's going to be clear skies all night.

Gemma Wonderful! **In that case**, I can't wait!

1. **barbecue** [ˈbɑrbɪkju] (n.) 烤肉
2. **forecast** [ˈforˌkæst] (n.) 預測；預報

phr. **in that case** 在這種情況下

▲ barbecue

82

烤肉

老龐：潔嫚，妳這中秋節已經有打算要做什麼了嗎？

潔嫚：還沒耶，你們要烤肉嗎？

老龐：對啊，我們要去公園，很歡迎妳加入我們。

潔嫚：太棒了，我很樂意參加，我要帶什麼食物或飲料嗎？

老龐：只要帶妳想喝的飲料就好，至於食物的話，我會買很多種食材，我們之後再分攤花費。

潔嫚：好啊，等等，中秋節是哪一天？是星期五嗎？

老龐：是啊。

潔嫚：你知道那天的天氣如何嗎？我記得去年都是雲雨，我們今年是否至少能看到月亮？

老龐：我看過氣象預告了，看來那天整晚都會是萬里無雲的好天氣。

潔嫚：太棒了，這樣的話，我可等不及了。

 Listening Practice 🎧 39

( ) **1.** What are the man and the woman talking about?

    a Going moon viewing.

    b Having a barbecue.

    c Making moon cakes.

    d Buying pomelos.

( ) **2.** What does the woman ask the man to do?

    a Make a list of ingredients.

    b Give her a ride to the store.

    c Call a friend for advice.

    d Check the weather forecast.

( ) **3.** Which of the following is the woman NOT going to get from the store?

    a Red bean paste.

    b Pineapples.

    c Sweet Potatoes.

    d Barbecue sauce.

Halloween
萬聖節

I Reading

Halloween, it could be argued, is the Western **equivalent**[1] of Taiwan's Ghost Festival. It's the night of the year when ghosts, **witches**,[2] monsters and all sorts of **terrifying**[3] creatures are said to **roam**[4] the earth. Unlike Ghost Festival, though, which generally has a serious **tone**,[5] Halloween is light-hearted. Children **dress up** in costumes and go around their neighborhoods knocking on doors and yelling "Trick or treat!" The grown-ups who open their doors to these little monsters **hand out** **fistfuls**[6] of candy in return for not being "tricked."

In the United States especially, people put a lot of effort into making Halloween as **spooky**[7] as possible. Walking around a neighborhood on October 31, you're likely to see houses decorated with many types of **creepy**[8] objects that are **guaranteed**[9] to send a chill down your **spine**.[10] The most classic Halloween decorations, though, are probably fake spiderwebs and jack-o'-lanterns (pumpkins **carved**[11] to **resemble**[12] scary faces and lit by placing candles inside).

▼ witch

Halloween is an ancient holiday, with a history of over 2000 years. It was originally celebrated by the Celts, who lived in Western Europe in pre-Christian times, as a festival marking the arrival of winter.

dress up ▶

1. **equivalent** [ɪˋkwɪvələnt] (n.) 相等物
2. **witch** [wɪtʃ] (n.) 女巫;巫婆
3. **terrifying** [ˋtɛrə͵faɪɪŋ] (a.) 令人害怕的
4. **roam** [rom] (v.) 漫遊;流浪
5. **tone** [ton] (n.) 調性
6. **fistful** [ˋfɪst͵fʊl] (n.) 一把
7. **spooky** [ˋspukɪ] (a.) 令人毛骨悚然的
8. **creepy** [ˋkripɪ] (a.) 不寒而慄的
9. **guarantee** [͵gærənˋti] (v.) 保證

10. **spine** [spaɪn] (n.) 脊柱;脊椎
11. **carve** [karv] (v.) 刻;雕刻
12. **resemble** [rɪˋzɛmbl] (v.) 像;類似

phr. **dress up** 裝扮
phr. **hand out** 發放

▲ trick or treat

萬聖節可說是相當於台灣中元節的西方節日,傳說每年的這天夜晚,鬼魂、女巫、怪物和各種駭人的生物會橫行遍地。不過不像中元節那般嚴肅,萬聖節的氣氛比較輕鬆愉快,兒童們會扮裝,到鄰居街坊敲門大喊「不給糖就搗蛋」,而替小怪物們開門的大人則會給他們一把糖果,以免被「搗蛋」。

特別在美國,人們會很努力地塑造萬聖節的恐怖氣氛。在十月 31 日這天到家附近走走,你很可能會看見用各種恐怖道具裝飾的房屋,必定會讓你寒毛直豎。不過,最經典的萬聖節裝飾,可能是假蜘蛛網和南瓜燈(人們把南瓜刻成嚇人的臉,並在裡面點上一盞燭火)。

萬聖節是個古老的節日,其歷史超過兩千年之久。萬聖節原本是凱爾特人慶祝的節日,他們在西元前住在西歐地區,用此節日慶祝冬日來臨。

This festival was called Samhain, and the Celts believed that during this time the **boundary**[13] between the living world and the spirit world would weaken. As a result, spirits would enter the **realm**[14] of the living to search for living bodies to **possess**.[15] Of course, the living did not want to be possessed, and so they dressed up in **ghoulish** costumes to make themselves as undesirable as possible.

During the first **millennium** AD, Christianity spread into Celtic lands, and the Church began to replace pagan holidays with Christian ones. In the 9th century, Pope Gregory IV declared November 1st All Hallows' Day, and so October 31st became known as All Hallows' Eve. This was later **contracted**[16] to Halloween.

▼ spooky Halloween skeleton

13. **boundary** [ˈbaʊndrɪ] (n.) 分界;界限
14. **realm** [rɛlm] (n.) 領域;範圍
15. **possess** [pəˈzɛs] (v.) 支配;附身
16. **contract** [kənˈtrækt] (v.) 縮小;濃縮

★ **ghoulish** [ˈɡulɪʃ] (a.) 食屍鬼似的
★ **millennium** [mɪˈlɛnɪəm] (n.) 千年

這個節日被稱為「萬聖夜」,凱爾特人相信在這個時刻,凡間與靈界的界線會減弱,因此,鬼魂會進到凡間,並尋找人的身體以依附。當然,人們並不想被附身,因此扮裝成厲鬼之樣,避免成為鬼魂的目標。

在西元一千年時,基督教傳進凱爾特地區,而教會開始用基督教節日取代異教節日。西元九世紀時,教宗額我略四世宣布 11 月一日為「諸聖節」,而十月 31 日則是「諸聖節前夕」,後來才濃縮成為萬聖節。

◀ fake spiderwebs

II Reading Comprehension Questions

(   ) **1.** Which of the following is commonly heard on Halloween?

- a Trick or trip!
- b Treat or trick!
- c Trick or treat!
- d Treat or trap!

(   ) **2.** Which of the following are houses often decorated with on Halloween?

- a Spiderwebs.
- b Costumes.
- c Candy.
- d Celtic symbols.

(   ) **3.** Which of these is used to light up a jack-o'-lantern according to the writer?

- a A candle.
- b A torch.
- c A laser.
- d A light bulb.

(   ) **4.** Which of these phrases is the word "Halloween" derived from?

- a All Hallows' Eve.
- b All Saints' Day.
- c All Hallows' Day.
- d Samhain.

(   ) **5.** What did the Celts do to avoid being possessed by the spirits?

- a Hide from them.
- b Dress up like ghosts.
- c Make loud noises.
- d Offer them candy.

DRESSING UP FOR HALLOWEEN

Tina What are you dressing up as this year for Halloween, Mark?

Mark I think I'm going to dress up as a **vampire**.

Tina A vampire? Didn't you do that last year?

Mark Yeah, but it's a classic Halloween look, and this way I don't have to buy a new costume.

Tina OK, but I think you should be more creative.

Mark Well, I'm open to suggestions.

Tina What about an **alien**,[1] or a **skeleton**,[2] or wait, a **werewolf**!

Mark I quite like the werewolf idea. Yeah, OK. I'll go to the Halloween store later and see if they have anything.

▲ alien

Tina Cool. I'll come with you. I need to pick out my costume, too.

Mark What are you going as?

Tina I was thinking of getting a princess costume and then using **makeup**[3] to make myself look a like a zombie princess!

▲ skeleton

Mark Nice! Very spooky!

1. **alien** [ˈelɪən] (n.) 外星人
2. **skeleton** [ˈskɛlətn̩] (n.) 骨骼；骨頭人
3. **makeup** [ˈmekˌʌp] (n.) 化妝品

★ **vampire** [ˈvæmpaɪr] (n.) 吸血鬼
★ **werewolf** [ˈwɪrˌwʊlf] (n.) 狼人

▲ vampire

◀ werewolf

為萬聖節扮裝

蒂娜：馬克，你今年萬聖節要打扮成什麼？
馬克：我想要打扮成吸血鬼。
蒂娜：吸血鬼？你去年不就這麼做了嗎？
馬克：是啊，但這是經典的萬聖節裝扮，而且這樣的話我就不
　　　用買新道具服了。
蒂娜：好吧，但我覺得你應該要更有創意。
馬克：嗯，我接受建議。
蒂娜：打扮成外星人如何，或是骷髏人，對了，打扮成狼人！
馬克：我蠻喜歡狼人這個主意，好，那我晚點會去萬聖節商店，
　　　看看他們有沒有賣。
蒂娜：真酷，那我要跟你去，我也需要挑選道具服。
馬克：妳要打扮成什麼？
蒂娜：我想要買一件公主服，然後化妝成殭屍的樣子！
馬克：太棒了，超恐怖的！

Ⅳ Listening Practice 🎧 42

(　　) **1.** What are the speakers talking about?
　　　ⓐ Choosing a Halloween costume.
　　　ⓑ Making a Halloween decoration.
　　　ⓒ Going trick-or-treating.
　　　ⓓ Hosting a Halloween party.

(　　) **2.** What are the speakers going to do later?
　　　ⓐ Spray cobwebs on their windows.
　　　ⓑ Put up a fake skeleton.
　　　ⓒ Make pumpkin pie.
　　　ⓓ Get their faces painted.

(　　) **3.** Which of the following items is NOT
mentioned in the conversation?
　　　ⓐ A candle.
　　　ⓑ A knife.
　　　ⓒ A pen.
　　　ⓓ Glue.

UNIT 15

Thanksgiving
感恩節

I Reading

43

Thanksgiving Day is celebrated **annually**[1] on the fourth Thursday of November. It's an opportunity for Americans to give thanks for all the good things in their lives and to remember the **hardships**[2] suffered by America's early **settlers**.[3]

A typical thanksgiving scene **consists of** a family sitting around a dinner table **laden**[4] with turkey, **mashed**[5] potatoes, cranberry sauce, corn, various fall vegetables, and pumpkin pie. Traditionally, a prayer of thanks **precedes**[6] the start of the meal. Then it's time to dig in!

The first Thanksgiving was held in 1621 by the members of the Plymouth Colony in what is now the state of Massachusetts. The settlers

(known as the **Pilgrims**[7]) had set sail for the New World on a ship called the Mayflower on September 6, 1620. They'd done so in order to **flee**[8] **religious**[9] **persecution**[10] in England. After 65 days at sea, they landed at Plymouth. The first winter for them was harsh and **devastating.**[11] Grain they brought from Europe wouldn't grow in the **soil**[12] of their new homeland, and many died of **starvation**[13] and sickness. Of the 110 Pilgrims that had arrived, only 50 **survived**[14] the first winter.

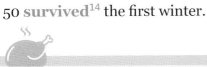
▼ mashed potatoes

turkey ▶

1. **annually** [ˈænjʊəlɪ] (adv.) 每年地
2. **hardship** [ˈhɑrdʃɪp] (n.) 艱難；困苦
3. **settler** [ˈsɛtlɚ] (n.) 移居者
4. **laden** [ˈledn̩] (a.) 裝滿的
5. **mashed** [mæʃt] (a.) 糊狀的
6. **precede** [priˈsid] (v.) 先於
7. **Pilgrim** [ˈpɪlgrɪm] (n.) 朝聖者
8. **flee** [fli] (v.) 逃走；逃離
9. **religious** [rɪˈlɪdʒəs] (a.) 宗教的；虔誠的

10. **persecution** [ˌpɜsɪˈkjuʃən] (n.) 迫害
11. **devastating** [ˈdɛvəsˌtetɪŋ] (a.) 毀滅性的；破壞性極大的
12. **soil** [sɔɪl] (n.) 土壤
13. **starvation** [starˈveʃən] (n.) 飢餓；餓死
14. **survive** [sɚˈvaɪv] (v.) 活下來；倖存

phr. **consist of** 由某事物組成或構成

▼ pumpkin pie

▲ cranberry sauce

感恩節每年於 11 月的第四個禮拜四舉行，對於美國人而言是個好機會，為生命中的所有美事致上感激之意，也同時紀念美國早期拓荒者的困苦。

典型的感恩節景象包括全家圍桌而坐，桌上放滿火雞、馬鈴薯泥、蔓越莓醬、玉米、各種秋季時蔬和南瓜派。根據傳統，在開動前會先做謝飯禱告，接著就是大快朵頤的時刻！

世界上的第一個感恩節於 1621 年，由普利茅斯殖民地的移民舉辦，普利茅斯殖民地是指現今的麻薩諸塞州。拓荒者（也稱為新移民）於 1620 年九月六日搭乘「五月花號」前往新大陸，他們這麼做是為了逃離英國的宗教迫害。他們在海上航行 65 日，並在普利茅斯登陸。他們遇上的第一個冬天非常艱辛困苦，從歐洲帶來的穀糧無法在新家園的土地上種植，許多人死於飢餓和疾病。當時總共有 110 位移民來到新大陸，卻只有 50 位活過這個冬季。

▲ the Mayflower

Seeing this, the local Native Americans came to the Pilgrims' rescue. They taught the Pilgrims skills for hunting and fishing. They also taught the Pilgrims how to plant corn and which plants were **poisonous**[15] and which had medicinal properties. With the newly **acquired**[16] knowledge, the harvest in the fall of 1621 was a great success. They had **sufficient**[17] corn, fruit, vegetables, fish, and meat to put away for the winter.

To celebrate the successful harvest, the Pilgrims held a three-day feast, complete with corn, barley, wild turkey, and **venison**. The Native Americans who had helped the Pilgrims survive their difficult first year were all invited, too.

The practice of celebrating Thanksgiving after harvest continued over the years. In 1941, Congress **proclaimed**[18] Thanksgiving Day a national holiday.

15. **poisonous** [ˋpɔɪzn̩əs] (a.) 有毒的；有害的
16. **acquire** [əˋkwaɪr] (v.) 獲得
17. **sufficient** [səˋfɪʃənt] (a.) 足夠的
18. **proclaim** [proˋklem] (v.) 聲明；宣布

★ **venison** [ˋvɛnəzn̩] (n.) 鹿肉

　　有鑑於此，當地的美洲原住民上前幫助新移民，他們教新移民狩獵和捕魚的技巧，他們也教新移民種植玉米的方式，以及分辨有毒植物和草藥的訣竅。透過這些新知識，1621 年秋季的收成大豐收，他們得到足夠的玉米、水果、蔬菜、魚和肉類，足以存糧過冬。

　　為了慶祝豐收，新移民舉辦了三日的盛宴，美食包括玉米、大麥、野火雞和鹿肉，他們也邀請所有曾在艱辛的第一年幫助他們的美洲原住民一同參與。

　　因豐收而慶祝感恩節的活動延續了好幾年，1941 年時，美國國會正式宣布感恩節為國定節日。

▲ prayer of thanks

II Reading Comprehension Questions

(   ) **1.** A traditional Thanksgiving dinner does NOT include which of the following?

   a Pizza.

   b Corn.

   c Pumpkin pie.

   d Turkey.

(   ) **2.** Why did the Pilgrims leave England?

   a They wanted to convert the Native Americans to Christianity.

   b They wanted to explore the New World.

   c They wanted to gain religious freedom.

   d They wanted to move to a warmer climate.

(   ) **3.** How many of the Pilgrims died during their first winter in the New World?

   a None.

   b One hundred and ten.

   c Over half of them.

   d Ninety percent of them.

(   ) **4.** What did the Native Americans teach the Pilgrims?

   a How to use poison.

   b How to speak their language.

   c How to hunt and fish.

   d How to make beer.

(   ) **5.** Which of the following is NOT true about the first Thanksgiving?

   a The local Indians were in attendance.

   b It lasted for three days.

   c It celebrated a successful harvest.

   d Only men were allowed to attend.

THANKSGIVING HOLIDAY SALES

Nicky I'm **setting**[1] the alarm clock for 3:00 a.m., OK?

Jake What? 3:00 a.m.! Why so early?

Nicky We have to be out of the house early tomorrow morning to **take advantage of** the holiday **sales**.[2] If we're smart, we can get all of our Christmas shopping done by tomorrow evening.

Jake But won't all the stores be closed that early in the morning?

Nicky No, silly. These days, on the day after Thanksgiving, all the stores open super early.

Jake Oh, great. But don't the sales **carry on** all weekend? Why are we **rushing**[3] to go tomorrow morning?

Nicky They used to, but now most stores stop their sales on Friday evening.

Jake Smart, that way everyone's so nervous about **missing out** that they all **pile in** on Friday morning.

Nicky Yep! It's going to be a real busy day tomorrow, so get some sleep. You'll need it.

1. **set** [sɛt] (v.) 設定
2. **sales** [selz] (n.) 銷售
3. **rush** [rʌʃ] (v.) 匆忙

phr. **take advantage of** 利用
phr. **carry on** 持續；繼續
phr. **miss out** 錯過
phr. **pile in** 湧進

▲ sales

感恩節特賣會

妮基：我把鬧鐘設在凌晨三點，這樣可以嗎？

傑克：什麼？凌晨三點！為什麼要這麼早？

妮基：我們明天早上得早點出門，才能搶到節日特賣。若我們夠聰明，我們可以在明晚前買好所有聖誕節的所需之物。

傑克：但店家在那麼早的時候還沒開吧？

妮基：才不呢，你好好笑，在這些日子，尤其是感恩節隔天，所有的店都超早開的。

傑克：喔太棒了，但特價不是會持續整個週末嗎？為什麼我們要趕在明天早上去？

妮基：以前是這樣，但現在大多數的店家星期五晚上就會結束特賣。

傑克：真聰明，這樣大家都會很緊張，怕錯過特賣，所以全都會在週五早上擠進商店。

妮基：沒錯，明天會是個忙碌的一天，所以你快睡吧，你明天會需要體力的。

 IV Listening Practice (45)

( ) **1.** What is the woman researching?

    [a] How to make turkey meat more flavorful.

    [b] How to choose the best turkey.

    [c] How to make turkey meat juicier.

    [d] How long to cook a turkey for.

( ) **2.** How long does the method chosen by the woman need to work?

    [a] A full day.

    [b] Two weeks.

    [c] Five minutes.

    [d] Three hours.

( ) **3.** Which of the following does the woman NOT need for her chosen method?

    [a] A fridge.

    [b] Salt.

    [c] A bowl of water.

    [d] Herbs and spices.

Christmas
聖誕節

I Reading

When you think of Christmas, what images spring to mind? For many, the **classic**[1] Christmas image is of Santa Claus climbing down the **chimney**[2] on Christmas **Eve**[3] and leaving gifts under a brightly lit Christmas tree.

However, Santa Claus, Christmas trees, and gift-giving are later additions to the Christmas tradition. They have little to do with the true origins of Christmas, which are religious in nature.

The original purpose of Christmas was to celebrate the birth of Jesus Christ, who is believed by Christians to be the son of God. The exact date of Christ's birth, however, is not mentioned in the **Bible**. In the Roman **pagan** calendar, late December was already a time of celebration, with several midwinter festivals **occurring**[4] at that time. The early Church may

Christmas ornaments ▶

have decided on December 25 as the date for Christmas simply because everyone was already used to celebrating at this time anyway.

Early in the Christmas season, many families decorate their homes with Christmas trees, **wreaths**,[5] and **ornaments**[6] in green and red, both traditional colors of Christmas.

1. **classic** [ˋklæsɪk] (a.) 典型的；經典的
2. **chimney** [ˋtʃɪmnɪ] (n.) 煙囪
3. **eve** [iv] (n.) 前夕
4. **occur** [əˋkɝ] (v.) 發生
5. **wreath** [riθ] (n.) 花圈
6. **ornament** [ˋɔrnəmənt] (n.) 裝飾品

★ **Bible** [ˋbaɪbl̩] (n.) 聖經
★ **pagan** [ˋpegən] (a.) 異教的

the birth of Jesus ▶

◀ Christmas wreath

當你想到聖誕節時，你腦海中會浮現出什麼樣的景象？對很多人而言，經典的聖誕節景象是聖誕老公公在聖誕夜從煙囪爬下來，並將禮物放在用亮燈布置的聖誕樹下。

然而聖誕老公公、聖誕樹和聖誕禮物都是後來才加進聖誕節傳統的事物，它們與聖誕節的真正起源不太相關，因為聖誕節本身其實是個宗教節日。

聖誕節原始的目的是用來慶祝耶穌的誕生，基督徒相信耶穌是神的兒子。然而，耶穌誕生的確切日期並沒有在《聖經》中載明。在羅馬異教徒的月曆中，12 月底本來就是慶祝的時刻，有許多冬季中期的節慶皆在此時舉辦。有可能早期教會決定把聖誕節定在 12 月 25 日，因為反正大家早已習慣在此時慶祝節慶。

在聖誕佳節的前幾天，家家戶戶會布置房子，用聖誕樹、聖誕花圈、以及紅色和綠色的聖誕飾品，因為這兩個顏色是聖誕節的傳統色。

◀ Santa Claus

Holly and **mistletoe** are also used for decorating. According to one tradition, any two people standing underneath **a sprig of** mistletoe should kiss. Therefore, if you're ever at a Christmas party, a good **rule of thumb** is to **stay** well **away from** the creepy guy holding the mistletoe!

Christmas ▶
stocking

On Christmas Eve in the United States, some people **attend**[7] church services, in which they listen to readings from the Bible and sing Christmas **carols**.[8] At home, kids hang up **stockings**[9] by the fireplace before going to bed and put out cookies and milk for Santa Claus, and a carrot for his **reindeer**.[10] On Christmas Day, people enjoy Christmas dinner, usually with **roast**[11] turkey as the main dish, as well as a host of other seasonal foods like **mince pies**, fruit cakes, and **eggnog**.

7. **attend** [əˋtɛnd] (v.) 參加
8. **carol** [ˋkærəl] (n.) 頌歌
9. **stocking** [ˋstɑkɪŋ] (n.) 長襪
10. **reindeer** [ˋrɛnˏdɪr] (n.) 馴鹿
11. **roast** [rost] (a.) 烘烤的

★ **mistletoe** [ˋmɪslˏto] (n.) 槲寄生
★ **mince pie** [mɪns paɪ] (n.) 肉餡餅
★ **eggnog** [ˋɛgˏnɑg] (n.) 蛋酒

▲ eggnog

▲ a sprig of mistletoe

phr. **a sprig of** 一束枝子
phr. **rule of thumb** 經驗法則
phr. **stay away from** 遠離……

東青和槲寄生也會被用來裝飾，有個常見的傳統是當兩人同時站在一束槲寄生下，他們必須彼此親吻。所以若你想參加聖誕派對，最佳的經驗法則就是遠離那位拿著槲寄生的詭異男子。

　　在美國的聖誕夜時，有些人會參加教會禮拜，他們會聆聽《聖經》的章節朗誦並唱聖誕歌，孩童會在睡前把襪子掛在火爐旁邊，為聖誕老公公準備餅乾和牛奶，且為他的馴鹿準備紅蘿蔔。聖誕節當天，人們會享用聖誕晚宴，通常主菜是烤火雞，加上其他許多當令食物，像是英式肉餡餅、水果餅和蛋酒。

◀ singing Christmas carol

II Reading Comprehension Questions

(   ) **1.** What can be inferred from the passage about mince pies, fruit cakes, and eggnog?

[a] They're bad for your health.

[b] They don't taste very good.

[c] They're usually eaten around Christmastime.

[d] They are usually eaten around the world.

(   ) **2.** According to the Bible, when was Jesus Christ born?

[a] On December 25.

[b] Sometime in December.

[c] The exact date is not mentioned.

[d] In early January.

(   ) **3.** What are the traditional colors of Christmas?

[a] Green and red.

[b] Green and white.

[c] Red and white.

[d] White and blue.

(   ) **4.** What are two people standing under a sprig of mistletoe expected to do?

[a] Shake hands.

[b] Kiss.

[c] Go on a date.

[d] Exchange gifts.

(   ) **5.** Which of the following is NOT a common Christmas Eve activity?

[a] Going to church.

[b] Hanging up a stocking.

[c] Putting out a plate of cookies.

[d] Planting a Christmas tree.

DECORATING A CHRISTMAS TREE

Joe   Paula! I've put up the Christmas tree. Have you got the decorations down from the **attic**[1]?

Paula   Yes. Here they are. Shall we start with the **tinsel**?

Joe   Great idea. You take the gold tinsel, and I'll take the red tinsel.

Paula   Nice. OK, now the **baubles**. Shall we just put red and gold ones on, to **match**[2] the tinsel? Or shall we just go all out.

Joe   Let's go all out. I think Christmas trees should be as colorful as possible.

Paula   OK, and now the lights. Careful not to get them **tangled**.[3]

Joe   Wow! That looks awesome. Oh, we forgot the tree-topper. Shall we put a star or an angel on the top of the tree?

Paula   I think an angel. We had a star last year.

Joe   There you go. Beautiful!

1. **attic** [ˈætɪk] (n.) 閣樓
2. **match** [mætʃ] (v.) 相配
3. **tangle** [ˈtæŋgl̩] (v.) 使糾結

★ **tinsel** [ˈtɪnsl̩] (n.) 金屬絲
★ **bauble** [ˈbɔbl̩] (n.) 小玩意兒

裝飾聖誕樹

喬：寶拉，我已經把聖誕樹架好了，妳把聖誕節裝飾從閣樓拿下來了嗎？

寶拉：拿了，在這裡，我們要從亮片銀絲開始布置嗎？

喬：好主意，妳拿金色的，我拿紅色的。

寶拉：很好，接著是小飾品。我們要不要只放紅色和金色的以搭配亮片？還是全部都放上去？

喬：我們全部都放上去吧，我覺得聖誕樹要盡量色彩繽紛。

寶拉：好，現在要放燈，小心不要把它們纏在一塊。

喬：哇！這看起來太棒了。喔，我們忘記樹頂裝飾了，我們要在樹頂上放星星還是天使？

寶拉：我覺得放天使好了，我們去年放過星星了。

喬：放好了，真美！

Ⅳ Listening Practice 🎧 48

( ) **1.** What does the woman asks the man to help her do?

    a Bake some gingerbread cookies.

    b Decorate some gingerbread cookies.

    c Sell some gingerbread cookies.

    d Eat some gingerbread cookies.

( ) **2.** What does the man find in the cupboard?

    a Edible glitter.

    b Chocolate buttons.

    c Sprinkles.

    d Green icing.

( ) **3.** What are the woman's cookies going to look like?

    a Reindeer.

    b Santa and his elves.

    c Stars.

    d Jesus Christ.

Listening Practice 錄音稿及譯文

 UNIT 1 P. 11

Ⓜ Hi, Jenny. Are you enjoying the party?

Ⓦ Hi, David. Yeah, it's great! Thanks for inviting me.

Ⓜ So have you decided who you're going to kiss at midnight?

Ⓦ Ha! I'm not sure. I guess we'll have to wait and see. By the way, someone said something about going up to the roof just before midnight to see the fireworks.

Ⓜ Yeah, we have a great view of the fireworks from our rooftop. You can see the whole show. Actually, what time is it now?

Ⓦ Gosh! It's 11:55 already! We'd better hurry up. Only five minutes to go!

🔵男 嗨，珍妮，妳在派對上玩得還開心嗎？

🔴女 嗨，大衛，很開心啊，這派對很棒，謝謝你邀請我。

🔵男 那麼妳決定午夜時要親誰了嗎？

🔴女 哈！我還不確定，我想我再看看好了。對了，有人說也許可以在午夜前去屋頂看煙火。

🔵男 是啊，我們家樓頂有極佳的視野可以看煙火，妳可以看到整場秀。對了，現在幾點了？

🔴女 天啊，已經 11 點 55 分了，我們最好動作快一點，只剩五分鐘了！

 UNIT 2 P. 17

Ⓜ Where are we going?

Ⓦ We're going to the temple to get a blessing. We need to make peace with the Year God.

Ⓜ Who's the Year God?

Ⓦ Well, there are 60 Year Gods altogether, and each year a different one rules over the year.

Ⓜ OK, but why do you have to make peace with him? Did you do something bad?

Ⓦ No, each year certain animals from the Chinese zodiac offend the Year God. If you were born under one of those signs, you need to go and get a blessing; otherwise, you'll have bad luck the whole year. You and I were both born in the Year of the Horse, so we need to get a blessing this year.

🔵男 我們要去哪裡？

🔴女 我們要去寺廟祈福，我們得去安太歲。

🔵男 太歲是誰？

🔴女 總共有 60 位太歲星君，每一年都由不同的太歲掌管。

🔵男 嗯，但為什麼妳需要去安太歲？妳有做錯什麼事嗎？

🔴女 沒有，每一年都有特定的生肖會與太歲相沖，若你的生辰屬於這些相沖的生肖，那麼你就得去安太歲，不然一整年將壞運連連。你和我都屬馬，所以我們今年必須安太歲。

UNIT
3 P. 23
🎧 09

Ⓜ Look over there, Jane. There are lanterns shaped like giant pieces of fruit! And over here are lanterns shaped like cartoon characters!

Ⓦ Amazing! I can't believe there are so many of them. And they're so big, too! They must be over three meters tall.

Ⓜ Let's go and see the main lantern. It's a giant rabbit.

Ⓦ Is that because it's the Year of the Rabbit this year?

Ⓜ Yes, the main lantern is always in the shape of the zodiac animal for that year. Next year, it'll be a gigantic dragon.

Ⓦ Oh my God! It's enormous and so colorful! It's taller than my house back home in Canada!

男 珍妮看那邊，那邊的燈籠形狀像是巨大的水果！還有這邊，那些燈籠的形狀是卡通人物！

女 太不可思議了，真不敢相信有這麼多燈籠，而且它們也都好大喔，一定有超過三公尺高。

男 我們去看主燈吧，是隻巨兔。

女 是因為今年是兔年嗎？

男 是啊，主燈的造型總是該年的生肖動物，明年將會是一隻巨龍。

女 喔我的天啊，真的超巨大的，而且色彩好豐富，比我加拿大的家還要高！

UNIT
4 P. 29
🎧 12

Ⓜ Angela, I need your advice.

Ⓦ OK, I'm listening.

Ⓜ Valentine's Day is coming up, and I want to do something special for my girlfriend. Do you have any suggestions?

Ⓦ Well, how about taking her away somewhere for the weekend? Maybe to a luxury hotel or something?

Ⓜ I think that's a bit out of my price range. I was thinking of something like making her a CD with romantic songs on it, except I did that last year.

Ⓦ You could write her a love poem. Just make sure it's not too lame.

Ⓜ That's not a bad idea, actually. Thanks, Angela.

男 安潔拉，我需要妳的建議。

女 好的，我在聽。

男 情人節快到了，我想為女友做些特別的事，妳有任何建議嗎？

女 嗯，你何不在那個週末帶她出去玩？也許去豪華旅館住之類的？

男 我覺得那有點超出我的預算，我是想幫她做一張浪漫歌曲的 CD 這類的，但我去年已經為她做過了。

女 你可以寫一首表達愛意的詩，但內容千萬不能太遜。

男 這主意其實還不錯，謝啦安潔拉。

🅜 Are you ready to go watch the parade, Jill? Hey! Why aren't you dressed up?

🅦 Dressed up? What do you mean?

🅜 It's St. Patrick's Day. You're supposed to be wearing green.

🅦 Yeah . . . Green's not really my color.

🅜 So what? It's a tradition. And what about the big green wig I gave you?

🅦 That? I thought that was a joke.

🅜 No. Come on, find something green to wear and put on the wig. Otherwise, you'll stand out like a sore thumb.

🅦 Fine, fine. Wait a second. What's that you're wearing around your shoulders?

🅜 It's a giant Irish flag. Now hurry up. The parade starts in 20 minutes.

🕒 吉兒，妳準備好要去看遊行了嗎？嘿！妳怎麼沒有打扮？

🕒 打扮？什麼意思？

🕒 今天是聖派屈克節，妳應該要穿綠色的服裝。

🕒 是喔……但我不太適合穿綠色的。

🕒 那又如何？這是傳統。妳何不戴我給妳的那頂綠色大假髮？

🕒 那個？我以為你是在捉弄我的耶。

🕒 才沒有呢，好啦，找件綠色的衣服穿然後戴上那頂假髮，不然妳會看起來特立獨行。

🕒 好啦好啦，等等，你肩膀上戴的那個東西是什麼？

🕒 是巨大的愛爾蘭國旗，妳快點啦，遊行再 20 分鐘後就要開始了。

🅦 I want to do something different this year for Easter.

🅜 What did you have in mind?

🅦 I thought it would be nice to decorate our own eggs this year.

🅜 You mean like they do in Eastern Europe?

🅦 Yeah. We can get some food coloring from the store and use it to dye our eggs different colors.

🅜 Cool! Is there anything else we need?

🅦 I looked online, and it said that if you add a little olive oil to the food coloring, you get a really cool swirling effect.

🅜 OK, so food coloring, olive oil . . .

🅦 And some white vinegar, too.

🅜 All right. Oh, and fresh eggs. Mustn't forget those!

🕒 我今年復活節想做點不一樣的事。

🕒 妳有什麼打算？

🕒 我想今年我們可以自己裝飾我們的蛋，這樣還不錯。

🕒 妳是說像東歐人那樣嗎？

🕒 是啊，我們可以從店裡買些食用顏料，用它把蛋染成不同顏色。

🕒 好酷，那麼我們還需要什麼嗎？

🕒 我上網查過了，它說若我們在食用顏料中加一些橄欖油，就能得到很酷的漩渦效果。

🕒 好，食用顏料、橄欖油……

🕒 還要一些白醋。

🕒 好的，喔，還有新鮮的蛋，一定不能忘了那些！

UNIT 7   P. 47 〔21〕

M It's almost Tomb Sweeping Day. We need to start preparing for our visit to my father's grave.

W OK. We need to buy some ghost money and some incense. I can get those later today.

M And we'll need some fresh fruit and flowers. Can you go to the market and pick some up?

W Yes, I'll put them on my list.

M Oh, and I'd like to offer something special, too. See if you can find a model of a nice car to burn.

W I think your father will really like that!

M I think so, too. And I'll get the tools for cleaning the grave out of the shed. I think a couple of weed removers and a broom should be enough.

男 清明節快到了,我們得開始準備去掃爸爸的墓。

女 好,我們要買一些紙錢和香,我今天晚一點可以去買。

男 我們也會需要一些新鮮水果和花,妳可以去菜市場買嗎?

女 好,我會將它們列在購物清單上。

男 喔,我也想給他一些特別的東西,看看妳能不能找一部不錯的汽車模型燒給他。

女 我想你爸應該會很喜歡。

男 我也這麼覺得,喔我也會從倉庫把掃墓的工具拿出來,我想一些除草工具和一支掃把應該就夠了。

UNIT 8   P. 53 〔24〕

W Where are we taking Mom for her Mother's Day dinner?

M I was thinking we could take her to the new Italian restaurant on Main Street.

W Good idea! She's been talking about that place for weeks. I'll call them now before they get booked up. Do you have their number?

M Yes, I do actually. I got their card when I was passing by yesterday. Here it is.

W Great. I'll book a table for the three of us at 7. Oh, wait. Do you think Johnny will be able to make it down from New York?

M I spoke to him yesterday. He said he's too busy, but he's sending some flowers for Mom.

女 我們要請媽去哪吃母親節晚餐?

男 我在想我們可以帶她去主要大街上那家新開的義大利餐廳。

女 好主意!她已經講那家餐廳講了好幾週了,我現在就打電話給餐廳免得被訂滿,你有餐廳電話嗎?

男 有啊,其實我昨天經過時有拿名片,給妳。

女 太好了,我會訂晚上七點三個人的位子。喔,等一下。你覺得強尼有可能從紐約來嗎?

男 我昨天跟他談過了,他說他太忙了,但他會送花給媽就是了。

M Lisa, I'm thinking of putting together a school rowing team for this year's Dragon Boat Festival. Do you want to join?

W Um, sure. I've never rowed before, but it sounds like fun. Who else were you thinking of?

M Well, I thought Pete might be interested.

W Yeah, he actually competed last year, so it'd be good to have someone with experience.

M Also, Tina. She used to row for England, so I think she'll definitely be in.

W Cool. How many people do we need for a team?

M Altogether we need 20 rowers, one drummer, and someone to steer.

W OK. I'll ask around. I think I know a few people in my class who'd be up for it.

男 麗莎，我想要為了今年的端午節組一支校園划船隊，妳想加入嗎？

女 呃，好啊，我從來沒划過船，但聽起來好像很好玩，你還想再找誰加入？

男 我覺得彼特應該會有興趣。

女 是啊，他去年其實有參賽過，能讓有經驗的人加入還不錯。

男 還有蒂娜，她以前在英國有在划船，所以我想她一定會加入。

女 好酷，那麼我們一隊需要多少人？

男 我們總共需要 20 位划船手，一位鼓手和一位舵手。

女 好，我會四處問問，我覺得我們班上應該會有一些人想參加。

W Hey, have you seen this in the local paper? It's a July Fourth singing competition.

M Let me see. Submit a video of yourself singing the national anthem. Wow! And the winner will get the chance to sing the anthem at the Independence Day fireworks show.

W How do they pick the winner?

M They post the videos on the newspaper's website and everyone votes on their favorite.

W Shall we enter? It might be fun.

M Well, I have a terrible voice, so I'm not going to. But you definitely should.

W OK. I'll go and get my camera and you can film me.

女 嘿，你在本地的報紙裡有看到這個嗎？是國慶日（七月四日）歌唱大賽。

男 我看看，請繳交您唱國歌的影片。哇，而且贏家可以得到在國慶日煙火秀時唱國歌的機會。

女 他們要怎麼選出贏家？

男 他們會在報紙官網上貼上影片，並讓大家選最喜歡的影片。

女 我們要參加嗎？應該會很好玩。

男 我唱歌超難聽的，所以我不會參加，但妳一定要參加。

女 好，我去拿照相機，你幫我錄影。

W James, can you give me a hand with the cooking, please?

M Sure. What are you cooking?

W Well, seeing as it's Father's Day, I thought I'd make your dad's favorite, steak and fries.

M Great, what do you want me to do?

W Can you chop those onions for me? And then season the steak with salt and pepper.

M No problem.

W Oh no! I forgot to buy potatoes. You can't make steak and fries without potatoes.

M It's OK. I'll run to the store and get some. We've still got an hour before Dad gets home.

W Thank you, Sweetie. You're an angel.

女 詹姆士,可以請你幫我煮菜嗎?

男 好啊,妳在煮什麼?

女 因為今天是父親節,我想說我可以煮你爸最愛的食物,牛排和薯條。

男 太棒了,那你要我做什麼呢?

女 你可以幫我切洋蔥嗎?然後用鹽和胡椒幫牛排調味。

男 沒問題。

女 喔不!我忘了去買馬鈴薯,沒有馬鈴薯就不能做牛排和薯條。

男 沒關係,我馬上去店裡買,離爸回到家還有一小時。

女 親愛的,謝謝你,你真是個救星。

W OK, honey, it's the fifteenth today. So let's start preparing the offerings table.

M What do we need to place first, Mom?

W First, we place the fruit offerings for the gods. Let's put three kinds of fruit: apples, oranges, and pineapples.

M OK, and how many of each kind?

W It has to be an odd number of each. So, three apples, five oranges, and three pineapples.

M OK, that's done. What next?

W Now we prepare the offerings for the wandering ghosts. We need three types of meat: chicken, fish, and pork.

M OK. Shall I just cut off a piece of the chicken and put it on the table?

W No, don't cut it. The chicken and the fish both need to be whole.

M We don't need a whole pig too, do we?

W No, just a chunk with a layer of skin, a layer of fat, and a layer of meat is enough.

女 好,親愛的,今天是初十五,我們來準備供桌吧。

男 媽,那我們需要先放上什麼呢?

女 首先,我們要放水果供品以祭拜神明,我們要放三種水果:蘋果、橘子和鳳梨。

男 好,那每種要放多少個?

女 數量必須都是奇數,所以放三顆蘋果、五顆橘子和三顆鳳梨。

男 好,放好了,然後呢?

女 然後我們要準備給好兄弟的供品,我們需要三種肉:雞肉、魚肉和豬肉。

男 好,那我要切一塊雞肉然後放在桌上嗎?

女 不,不要切,雞肉和魚肉必須都是完整的。

男 我們不需要放一整隻豬對吧?

女 不用,只要一塊包含豬皮、脂肪和豬肉的肉塊即可。

Ⓜ Hey, how about for Moon Festival this year we make our own moon cakes?

Ⓦ What a great idea. Do you know how to make them?

Ⓜ Yes, my mom taught me when I was younger.

Ⓦ OK, tell me what ingredients we need, and I'll go pick them up from the store.

Ⓜ For the crust we need flour, milk powder, baking powder, salt, eggs, sugar, and butter.

Ⓦ OK. Can you write that down for me?

Ⓜ Sure. What about the filling? Shall we just do the traditional red bean paste?

Ⓦ Um . . . Let's do some others as well. Maybe pineapple?

Ⓜ All right. How about sweet potato, too?

Ⓦ Lovely.

男 嘿，妳覺得今年中秋節我們自己來做月餅如何？

女 這主意太棒了，你知道月餅要怎麼做嗎？

男 我知道，我媽在我小時候時有教我。

女 好，告訴我，我們需要什麼食材，我去店裡買。

男 餅皮的話，我們需要麵粉、奶粉、泡打粉、鹽巴、雞蛋、糖和奶油。

女 好，你可以幫我寫下來嗎？

男 好的，那麼餡料呢？我們要用傳統的紅豆餡嗎？

女 嗯……我們也做一些別種的口味，也許鳳梨餡？

男 好啊，那麼番薯餡呢？

女 也不錯啊。

Ⓜ OK, so are you ready to make a jack-'o-lantern?

Ⓦ Yes! I've got our pumpkin here. What do we do first?

Ⓜ First we need to hollow out the pumpkin. So take this bread knife, and cut off a lid on the top.

Ⓦ OK. And now we just scoop out the insides?

Ⓜ That's right. Later, we'll make pumpkin pie with the filling.

Ⓦ Right. I've hollowed out the pumpkin. Now what?

Ⓜ It's simple. Just draw a scary face on the pumpkin with this marker, and cut out the shape.

Ⓦ Done! Now we just have to put the candle inside and light it, right?

Ⓜ Yep! And there you have it! A spooky jack-o'-lantern!

男 好，妳準備好要做南瓜燈了嗎？

女 準備好了！我已經準備好南瓜，我們先要怎麼做？

男 首先，我們要把南瓜挖空，拿著這把麵包刀，在上方切一個開口。

女 好，然後我們只要把裡面的東西挖出來嗎？

男 沒錯，我們之後可以會用餡做南瓜派。

女 好，我已經把南瓜挖空了，然後呢？

男 很簡單，只要用這支馬克筆在南瓜上畫一張恐怖的臉，接著切出形狀。

女 好了，然後我們現在只要把蠟燭放進去再點亮就好了對吧？

男 沒錯，這樣就完成了，一個可怕的南瓜燈。

UNIT
15 P. 95   🎧 45

M Hey, what are you doing?	**男** 嘿，你在幹嘛？
W I'm looking on the Internet for roast turkey recipes for Thanksgiving.	**女** 我在上網找感恩節烤火雞的食譜。
M I love the way you cook turkey, though.	**男** 但我喜歡妳料理火雞的方式。
W Aw, thanks honey. But I want to see if I can get the meat a little more juicy.	**女** 感謝你親愛的，但我想看看我能不能讓肉再多汁一點。
M What have you found so far?	**男** 妳現在找到了什麼？
W Well, according to this website, soaking the turkey in salt water for 24 hours before cooking will make the meat much juicier.	**女** 根據這個網站，在烤火雞前把火雞浸在鹽水中 24 小時會讓火雞更多汁。
M That's a good tip, and pretty easy to do, too. We just need a big bowl of water and some salt, right?	**男** 那真是個好點子，也很容易做到，我們只需要一大碗水和一些鹽對吧？
W Pretty much. Then we just leave it in the fridge to soak. OK, let's try it.	**女** 差不多，然後我們就只要把它放在冰箱裡浸泡。好，我們來試試。

UNIT
16 P. 101   🎧 48

W Henry, do you want to help me decorate these gingerbread cookies?	**女** 亨利，你想幫我裝飾這些薑餅嗎？
M Yeah! I'd love to.	**男** 好啊，我很樂意。
W OK. Well, I've got two kinds. Some are in the shape of Christmas trees, and others are in the shape of people.	**女** 好的，我有兩種餅乾，一種是聖誕樹形狀的，另一種是人的形狀。
M Can I decorate the Christmas tree cookies?	**男** 我可以裝飾聖誕樹形狀的餅乾嗎？
W Sure. I have some green icing here, some sprinkles, and some chocolate buttons.	**女** 可以啊，我有一些綠色糖衣、糖粉和一些巧克力鈕扣。
M Great. Do you have any edible glitter?	**男** 太好了，妳有可食用的亮粉嗎？
W I think so. Check in the cupboard over there.	**女** 好像有，你去那邊的櫃子看看。
M Yeah! I found it.	**男** 耶！我找到了。
W Good. You decorate the trees, and I'll decorate the people.	**女** 很好，你裝飾聖誕樹餅乾，我裝飾人物餅乾。
M You should decorate one as Santa and the others as his elves.	**男** 你應該做一個聖誕老人，然後其他是他的小精靈。
W Great idea, Henry!	**女** 亨利，這主意太棒了。

Answer Key 解答

Unit 1
II. 1. c   2. c   3. d   4. b   5. a   P. 9

IV. 1. d   2. a   3. b   🎧 03   P. 11

Unit 2
II. 1. b   2. a   3. c   4. c   5. d   P. 15

IV. 1. a   2. b   3. c   🎧 06   P. 17

Unit 3
II. 1. c   2. b   3. a   4. b   5. c   P. 21

IV. 1. b   2. c   3. c   🎧 09   P. 23

Unit 4
II. 1. a   2. b   3. b   4. b   5. d   P. 27

IV. 1. b   2. c   3. b   🎧 12   P. 29

Unit 5
II. 1. b   2. c   3. a   4. c   5. a   P. 33

IV. 1. c   2. d   3. b   🎧 15   P. 35

Unit 6
II. 1. c   2. b   3. a   4. c   5. b   P. 39

IV. 1. c   2. b   3. a   🎧 18   P. 41

Unit 7
II. 1. c   2. d   3. a   4. b   5. a   P. 45

IV. 1. a   2. d   3. b   🎧 21   P. 47

Unit 8
II. 1. d   2. a   3. b   4. c   5. a   P. 51

IV. 1. a   2. c   3. d   🎧 24   P. 53

Unit 9
II. 1. b   2. c   3. a   4. c   5. a   P. 57

IV. 1. b   2. c   3. c   🎧 27   P. 59

Unit 10
II. 1. a   2. b   3. b   4. a   5. c   P. 63

IV. 1. b   2. a   3. c   🎧 30   P. 65

Unit 11
II. 1. a   2. b   3. a   4. c   5. c   P. 69

IV. 1. c   2. a   3. b   🎧 33   P. 71

Unit 12
II. 1. a   2. b   3. a   4. d   5. b   P. 75

IV. 1. a   2. a   3. d   🎧 36   P. 77

Unit 13
II. 1. b   2. d   3. d   4. a   5. a   P. 81

IV. 1. c   2. a   3. d   🎧 39   P. 83

Unit 14
II. 1. c   2. a   3. a   4. a   5. b   P. 87

IV. 1. b   2. c   3. d   🎧 42   P. 89

Unit 15
II. 1. a   2. c   3. c   4. c   5. d   P. 93

IV. 1. c   2. a   3. d   🎧 45   P. 95

Unit 16
II. 1. c   2. c   3. a   4. b   5. d   P. 99

IV. 1. b   2. a   3. b   🎧 48   P. 101